The Heat's On

Chester Himes was born in 1909 in Jefferson City, Missouri. After being expelled from university he was convicted of armed robbery at the age of nineteen and sentenced to twenty to twenty five years' hard labour. It was while in jail (he was eventually released on parole after seven and a half years) that Himes started to write, publishing stories in a number of magazines, including *Esquire*. He then took a series of manual jobs while still writing. He published his first novel, *If He Hollers Let Him Go*, in 1945. A humiliating stint as a Hollywood scriptwriter ended in his being fired on racial grounds – as he wrote later, he felt he survived undamaged the earlier disasters in his life but it was 'under the mental corrosion of race prejudice in Los Angeles I became bitter and saturated with hate'.

Himes moved to Paris in 1953: a city that he – like many African-American writers of his generation – found sympathetic and stimulating. He lived much of the rest of his life first in France and then in Spain, where he moved in 1969. A meeting with Marcel Duhamel, the editor of Gallimard's crime list, 'La Série Noire', resulted in Himes being commissioned to write what became *La Reine des pommes*, published in English in 1957 as *For Love of Imabelle* or *A Rage in Harlem*, and which won the Grand Prix de la Littérature Policière. This was the first of the Harlem novels that were to make Himes famous and was followed by further titles, each translated first into French and then published in English, including *The Real Cool Killers*, *All Shot Up*, *The Heat's On* and *Cotton Comes to Harlem*. Himes was married twice. He died in Spain in 1984.

Noel 'Razor' S~~~~~~~~~~~~~~~~~~~~~~~~~~~~~~~~ He has fifty-eight criminal con~~~~~~~~~~~~~~~~~~~~~~~~~~~~~~ve years of a life sentence for ~~~~~~~~~~~~~~~~~~~~~~~~~~~~eived an Honours Diploma fro~~~~~~~~~~~~~~~~~~~~~~~~~~ok an AS level in Law and gain~~~~~~~~~~~~~~~~~~~~~~~~~~writing. He is the author of *A F~~~~~~~~~~~~~~~~~~~~Warrior Kings* and *A Rusty Gun*.

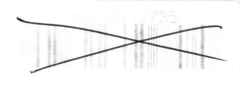

CHESTER HIMES

The Heat's On

With an introduction by Noel 'Razor' Smith

PENGUIN BOOKS

PENGUIN CLASSICS

Published by the Penguin Group
Penguin Books Ltd, 80 Strand, London WC2R ORL, England
Penguin Group (USA) Inc., 375 Hudson Street, New York, New York 10014, USA
Penguin Group (Canada), 90 Eglinton Avenue East, Suite 700, Toronto, Ontario, Canada M4P 2Y3
(a division of Pearson Penguin Canada Inc.)
Penguin Ireland, 25 St Stephen's Green, Dublin 2, Ireland (a division of Penguin Books Ltd)
Penguin Group (Australia), 250 Camberwell Road, Camberwell, Victoria 3124, Australia
(a division of Pearson Australia Group Pty Ltd)
Penguin Books India Pvt Ltd, 11 Community Centre, Panchsheel Park, New Delhi – 110 017, India
Penguin Group (NZ), 67 Apollo Drive, Rosedale, Auckland 0632, New Zealand
(a division of Pearson New Zealand Ltd)
Penguin Books (South Africa) (Pty) Ltd, 24 Sturdee Avenue, Rosebank, Johannesburg 2196, South Africa

Penguin Books Ltd, Registered Offices: 80 Strand, London WC2R ORL, England

www.penguin.com

First published in France as *Ne nous énervons pas* in 1961 and in the USA as *The Heat's On* in 1966
Published in Penguin Classics 2011

1

Copyright © Chester Himes, 1966
Introduction copyright © Noel 'Razor' Smith, 2011
All rights reserved

The moral right of the introducer has been asserted

Set in 11.25/14 pt Monotype Dante
Typeset by Ellipsis Digital Limited, Glasgow
Printed in England by Clays Ltd, St Ives plc

978-0-141-19647-3

www.greenpenguin.co.uk

Penguin Books is committed to a sustainable
future for our business, our readers and our
planet. This book is made from paper certified
by the Forest Stewardship Council.

Introduction

I first came across the novels of Chester Himes back in the mid-1970s when I was serving a Borstal sentence and had just learned to read. My hunger for good, entertaining fiction was all consuming, but the choice of reading material available to me was very limited in an institution where even our letters were censored by a matron – an ex-policewoman who went as far as to rip Page Three out of the daily tabloid lest we all masturbate ourselves to blindness. The books that were deemed 'suitable' reading for our youthful minds could not contain swearing, sex, or violence in any form (even Agatha Christie novels were banned because each one contained at least one murder!), which left us fourteen-to twenty-one-year-olds facing a pretty bleak time of it on the reading front. Fortunately there was a black-market trade in paperbacks, smuggled into the jail and with their usually lurid and giveaway covers removed, known as 'floaters'. Floaters would be passed around from reader to reader away from the gimlet gaze of the screws and matron, and sometimes, if a book was deemed particularly good, there would be a small charge for the privilege of reading it. One such book that usually incurred a charge – two roll-ups, if I remember rightly – was Chester Himes's *The Heat's On*.

The Heat's On was just the kind of novel that the authorities didn't want us getting hold of. It was fast, exciting, and full of the kind of characters that a street kid from Brixton – which I was – would find pretty familiar. And, of course, it was packed with violence and profanity, though a little short of sex. The phrase 'mother-raper', which the characters use throughout the story and which I assume Himes had to use instead of the more profane 'mother-fucker', would have had the Borstal matron reaching for her Bible, smelling salts and scissors. But the book came highly recommended by the discerning readers of B-wing so I paid my two precious roll-ups and hurried back to my cell with it tucked inside my jacket.

From the first page – the conversation between Pinky, the giant albino, and Jake, the heroin-dealing dwarf – I was hooked like a tea head with a major Jones. The world that Himes took me to was both familiar and fascinating. Violent cops who weren't averse to planting evidence and roughing up suspects if they thought the end justified the means, drug-dealing low-lifes and petty criminals of every hue and creed – to me it was like coming home. Even at that age – seventeen – I knew that Himes was a 'real' writer, someone who knew the score out on the streets and not just someone with no knowledge or experience trying to wing it. The writing of Chester Himes spoke to me personally and made me realize that books didn't have to be dry and boring, reading could be an absolute pleasure if you got the right book – and *The Heat's On* was definitely the right book.

First published in 1966, *The Heat's On* featured Himes's main characters – the Harlem detectives Grave Digger Jones and Coffin Ed Johnson – the first real anti-heroes I ever came across. I had mixed feelings about them. On the one hand they were upholding the rule of law in a difficult situation, shrugging off casual racism on a daily basis, so by rights they should have been the 'goodies', but on the other hand they were overly rough – bordering on brutal – with almost everyone on their beat. The people of Harlem are terrified of this gruesome twosome, and I must say with some justification. People are for ever being threatened, pistol-whipped, and punched about by Grave Digger and Coffin Ed, which made them more like the coppers I'd had dealings with. Though they are essentially on the side of right, still, these guys make Regan and Carter look like a pair of Jehovah's Witnesses. For me there are so many more interesting characters among the real villains – Uncle Saint, the shotgun-wielding chauffeur-bodyguard and ventriloquist – Sister Heavenly, the drug-dealing, marijuana-smoking, ruthless killer and, of course, Pinky, the giant albino dope fiend. Himes's characters are many faceted, never one dimensional, and his dialogue is spot on and a joy to read.

By the time I'd finished *The Heat's On* I wanted to read more Himes books. Unfortunately it was to be another three years before I got the chance to renew my acquaintance with the fiction of Mr Himes – this time it was *The Real Cool Killers*. But it wasn't until much later that I learned a bit about the man himself. Coming from a respectable middle-class family he grew up in Missouri and Ohio, his father was a college professor and his mother a teacher in a seminary, and Himes spent some time in college himself before being expelled in 1929. At the age of nineteen Himes had been arrested, beaten by the police and sentenced to twenty-five years' hard labour for armed robbery. He served seven and a half years before being released, and it was whilst he was serving this sentence that he began to write and had his first short stories published. I have no doubt that his experiences in prison and the characters he would have met there coloured his writing, and in particular his crime novels. Himes had been to prison, lived through the Great Depression, and knew exactly what it was like to be a black man living in a white-run society long before the civil rights movement in America, and these experiences are there in his writing. As he said in his autobiography, *The Quality of Hurt* (1973) – 'Up to the age of thirty-one I had been hurt emotionally, spiritually, and physically as much as thirty-one years could bear.' That he could channel this pain and misery into some of the greatest crime novels ever written is a testament to his skill as a writer and his spirit as a man.

If this is the first Chester Himes novel you've picked up, then believe me, you are in for a treat.

Noel 'Razor' Smith

I

'You're my friend, ain't you?' the giant asked.

He had a voice that whined like a round saw cutting through a pine knot.

'What do you need with a friend, as big as you are?' the dwarf kidded.

'I is asking you,' the giant insisted.

He was a milk-white albino with pink eyes, battered lips, cauliflowered ears and thick, kinky, cream-colored hair. He wore a white T-shirt, greasy black pants held up with a length of hemp rope, and blue canvas rubber-soled sneakers.

The dwarf put on an expression of hypocritical solicitude. He flicked back his sleeve and glanced at the luminous dial on his watch. It was 1:22 a.m. He relaxed. There was no need to hurry.

He was a hunchback with a dirty yellow complexion, shades darker than that of the albino. Beady black eyes that could not focus on anything looked out from a ratlike face. But he was dressed in an expensive blue linen, handstitched suit, silk-topped shoes and a black panama hat with a dull orange band.

His shifty gaze flicked for a moment on the rope knot at the giant's belly, which was on a level with his own eyes. The giant could make four of him, but he was not scared. The giant was just another sucker as far as he was concerned.

'You know I'm your friend, daddy-o. I'm old Jake. I'm your

real cool friend.' He spoke in a wheezing voice that was accustomed to whispering.

The giant's battered white face knotted into a frown. He looked up and down the dimly lit block on Riverside Drive.

On one side was a wall of big dark buildings. Not one lighted window was visible. On the other side was a park. He could make out the shapes of trees and benches, but he could only smell the flowers and the recently watered grass. A block away was the squat dark shape of Grant's Tomb.

None of that interested him.

The park sloped sharply to the West Side Highway. He saw the scattered lights of late motorists going north toward Westchester County. Beyond the highway was the Hudson River, flickering vaguely in the dark. Across a mile of water was the New Jersey shore. It might have been the Roman walls for all he cared.

He put his ham-size hand on the dwarf's small bony shoulder. The dwarf's back seemed to bend.

'Don't give me that stuff,' he said. 'I don't mean no real cool friend. You is everybody's real cool friend. I mean is you my sure enough, really and truly friend?'

The dwarf wriggled irritably beneath the weight of the giant's hand. His shifty gaze traveled up the huge white arm and lit on the giant's thick white neck. Suddenly he realized that he was alone with a giant halfwit on a dark deserted street.

'Look here, Pinky, ain't Jake always been your friend?' he said, pumping earnestness into his wheezing whisper.

The giant blinked like a dull mind reacting to a sudden apparition. Knobs of scar tissue shading his pink eyes moved like agitated lugworms. His cauliflowered ears twitched. His thick scarred lips drew back in a grimace. Rows of gold-crowned teeth flashed like a beacon in the semidark.

'I don't mean no always-been-your-friend friend,' he whined angrily, his grip tightening involuntarily on the dwarf's shoulder.

The dwarf winced with pain. His gaze flicked up toward the giant's agitated face; but it bounced right off. It lighted for a moment on the twenty-two-story tower of the Riverside Church, rising in the dark behind the giant's back. He became increasingly apprehensive.

'I mean is you my friend through thick and thin?' the giant insisted. 'Is you my friend through smoke and fire?'

The sound of a fire engine sounded faintly from the distance.

The dwarf heard it . . . *smoke and fire* . . . He began to get the connection. He struggled to break from the giant's grip.

'Turn me loose, fool!' he cried. 'I got to split.'

But the giant held on to him. 'Can't split now. You got to stay and back me up. You got to tell 'em for me, friend.'

'Tell who what, you fool?'

'The firemen, thass who. You got to tell 'em how my pa is gonna get robbed and murdered.'

'Shit!' the dwarf said, trying to push the giant's hand from his shoulder. 'Ain't nothing going to happen to Gus, you mother-raping idiot!'

But the giant only tightened his grip; his first finger and thumb closed about the dwarf's neck.

The dwarf squirmed like a pig in a sack, becoming panic-stricken; his beady black eyes bulged from their sockets. He hammered at the giant's thick torso with his puny fists.

'Turn me loose, you big mother-raper!' he screamed. 'Can't you hear those sirens? Are you stone-deaf? We can't be seen together on this plushy street. We'll get nabbed for sure. I'm a three-time loser. I'll get life in prison.'

The giant leaned forward and pushed his face before the face of the dwarf. The scar tissue on his blurred white face seemed to be jumping with a life of its own, like snakes in a hot fire. His body trembled and his nostrils flared and his eyes gleamed like pink coals as he stared into the beady black eyes of the dwarf.

'Thass why I been asking is you my friend through thick and thin,' he whined in a desperately urgent whisper.

The quiet environs of Riverside Drive were shattered with ear-splitting noise as fire engines and police cruisers poured into the street.

The dwarf stopped beating futilely at the giant's torso and began frantically to fish little square paper packets from his own pockets and eat them up. He stuffed them into his mouth, one after another, chewed desperately and swallowed. His face turned purple as he began to choke.

At the same instant, firemen jumped from the still-moving engines and rushed toward the church, brandishing axes. Some burst through the front doors and rushed about in the black dark 215-foot nave, stumbling over pews and banging into pillars, looking for burning timbers to chop away. Others rushed around the sides of the building, searching for other accesses.

The fire captain was already in the street, shouting orders through his megaphone.

A church sexton came from a dark recess beside the huge front doors where he had been hiding.

He leveled an accusing finger at the giant albino and cried, 'There's the man who put in the false alarm!'

The captain saw him but could not hear him. 'Get that civilian out of the danger zone!' he shouted.

Two prowl car cops on the alert for trouble rushed forward and seized the sexton.

'All right, buddy, get back,' one of them ordered.

'I am trying to tell you,' the sexton said through gritted teeth. 'That big man there put in the fire alarm.'

The cops released the sexton and turned toward the giant.

'What's going on here? Why are you choking that shrimp?' the vocal one asked in a hard voice.

'He's my friend,' the giant whined.

The cop reddened with anger.

The dwarf gurgled as though choking and his eyes popped.

The cop looked from one to the other, trying to decide which one to slug. They both looked guilty, he had no choice.

'Which one of you guys put in the alarm?' he asked.

'He did,' the sexton said, pointing at the giant.

The cop looked at the giant and decided to call the fire captain. 'We got the man who put in the alarm, sir.'

The fire captain called back, 'Ask him where the fire is!'

'Fire?' the giant said as though he didn't know what it was.

'Fire!' the sexton echoed in outrage. 'There isn't any fire! That's what I been trying to tell you.'

The two cops looked at one another. All these fire engines and no fire, they thought. Suddenly one was reminded of that song by Louis Armstrong, 'All that meat and no potatoes . . .'

But the fire captain purpled with rage. He moved toward the giant with balled fists.

'Did you put in the alarm?' he asked dangerously, his chin jutting forward.

The giant released his grip on the dwarf and said, 'You tell him, Jake.'

The dwarf tried to run but one of the cops caught him by the neck of his coat collar.

'I saw him when he did it,' the sexton said.

The captain wheeled on him. 'Why didn't you stop him? Do you know what it costs the city to put all these engines into operation?'

'Hell, look at him,' the sexton replied. 'Would you have stopped him?'

They all looked at him. They understood what the sexton meant. One of the cops flashed his light into the giant's face to see him better. He saw the white face with the Negroid features and white hair. He had never seen an albino Negro. He was astonished.

'What the hell are you?' he asked.

'I'm his friend,' the giant said, pointing at the dwarf struggling in the other cop's grip.

The captain's eyes stretched. 'By God, he's a nigger!' he exclaimed.

'Well, kiss my foot!' the first cop said. 'I thought there was something damn funny about him to be a white man.'

The dwarf took advantage of the distraction and broke from the other cop's grip. He ran around the rear of the fire captain's car and started across the street.

Brakes squealed and a fast-moving car slewed sidewise to keep from running him down.

Two big loose-jointed colored men wearing dark battered felt hats and wrinkled black alpaca suits emerged in unison from opposite sides of the front seat and hit the pavement in identical flat-footed lopes.

They came around the front of their little black sedan and converged on the running dwarf. Coffin Ed reached out a hand and caught hold of a thin, bony arm. It felt as though it might break off in his hand. He spun the hunchback around.

'It's Jake,' Grave Digger said.

'Look at his face,' Coffin Ed said.

'He's been eating it,' Grave Digger observed.

'But he ain't digested it yet,' Coffin Ed concluded, gripping the dwarf from behind by both arms.

Grave Digger hit the dwarf in the stomach.

The dwarf doubled over and began to vomit.

Grave Digger took out a handkerchief and spread it on the ground so that the dwarf vomited into it.

Half-chewed packets of paper came out with bits of boiled tongue and dill pickle.

Suddenly the dwarf fainted. Coffin Ed carried him over to the edge of the street and laid him on the grass border.

Grave Digger carefully folded the vomit-filled handkerchief and inserted it into a heavy manila envelope which he stuck into his leather-lined side coat pocket.

They left the dwarf lying on the ground and moved over to see what the commotion was about.

The giant was saying to the fire captain, 'Jake can tell you, boss. He's my friend.'

'Jake ain't talking,' Grave Digger said.

The giant looked stunned.

'He's a halfwit,' one of the white cops said.

By now the giant was encircled by several cops and a number of firemen.

'Halfwit or not, he's going to answer my question,' the captain said, pinning his bloodshot gaze onto the giant's pink eyes. 'Why did you ring the fire alarm, boy?'

Sweat flowed down the giant's cheeks like tears.

'Boss, I didn't go to start all this,' he whined. 'All I wanted was for somebody to come and stop 'em from robbing and murdering my pa.'

Grave Digger and Coffin Ed tensed.

'Where at?' Grave Digger asked.

'He works for the janitor of the apartment house three doors up the street,' the sexton volunteered.

'He's my pa,' the giant said.

'Shut up, all of you, and let me ask the questions,' the fire captain grated. He leaned toward the giant. He was over six feet tall but he only came up to the level of the giant's flat nose. 'I want to know why you came here and rang the special fire alarm for Riverside Church?' he insisted. 'You're not such an idiot that you don't know there is a special fire alarm just for this famous church.'

'He told you,' Coffin Ed said.

The fire captain ignored him. His teeth clenched so fiercely the muscles knotted in his purple-tinted jaws. 'Why didn't you phone the police? Why didn't you put in a police alarm? Why didn't you ring some other fire alarm? Why didn't you just yell for help?'

The giant looked bewildered. His flat white face began twitching. He licked a pink tongue across colorless lips.

'It was the closest,' he said.

'Closest to what?' the fire captain rasped.

'Closest to where he lives, obviously,' Grave Digger said.

'This is my business!' the fire captain shouted. 'You keep out.'

'If it's murder or robbery it's our business,' Grave Digger replied.

'Do you believe this idiot?' a white cop asked scornfully.

'It won't take long to find out,' Coffin Ed said.

'I'm going to find out first why he rang this alarm and got all these engines out here,' the fire captain said.

He reached forward with his left hand to clutch the giant in a vise, but he didn't find any place to take hold. The giant's T-shirt was too flimsy and his sweaty white skin was too slippery. So the fire captain just held out his hand with the palm forward as though to push the giant in the chest.

'Who's trying to rob your pa?' Grave Digger asked quickly.

'There's an African and my stepma; they is teaming up on him,' the giant whined.

The fire captain rapped him on the chest. 'But you knew there wasn't any fire.'

The giant looked about for help. There wasn't any.

'Nawauh, boss, I didn't exactly know there wasn't any fire,' he denied. He glanced at the captain's face and admitted, 'But I didn't seen any.'

The fire captain blew his top. He hit the giant in the stomach with all his might. His fist bounced back as though he had hit the tire of a truck.

The giant looked surprised.

'There ain't no need of that,' Coffin Ed said. 'He's willing to talk.'

The fire captain ignored him. 'Let's take him, boys,' he said.

A fireman took hold of the giant's right arm while the fire captain looped a left into his hard rubber stomach.

The giant grunted. He reached out his left hand and took the captain by the throat.

'Easy does it!' Grave Digger shouted. 'Don't make graves.'

'Keep out of this,' a white cop warned him, drawing his police revolver.

The captain's eyes bulged and his purpling tongue popped out.

A fireman hit the giant in the back with the flat of his ax. A sound came from the giant's mouth like a wet cough.

Another fireman raised his ax.

Grave Digger caught it by the handle in midstroke and drew his long-barreled, nickel-plated, .38-caliber revolver. He swung the barrel against the back of the giant's hand. The pain went through the giant's hand into the captain's Adam's apple and the captain's head filled with a shower of blue-pointed stars.

The giant's grip went slack and the captain fell.

At the sight of the captain on the ground, tempers flared.

The fireman snatched his ax from Grave Digger's grasp and made as though to chop at him.

From the other side, Coffin Ed's revolver flashed in the dim light as he warned, 'Don't do it. Don't lose your head. Your ass goes with it.'

The fireman whirled his ax and hit the giant a glancing blow across the back of the neck.

The giant cried like an enraged stallion and began to fight. He elbowed the fireman on his right in the jaw, knocking him unconscious. He couldn't close his left hand, but he flailed out with his left arm and flattened two firemen with axes.

Firemen reversed their axes and began whaling at him with the hickory handles. Some were getting through and making deep purple welts on the giant's sensitive white skin. Firemen were going down from the giant's pumping right fist and bodies were piling up as though a massacre were taking place. Still others closed in. The giant showed no signs of weakening, but he was slowly turning black and blue.

The sexton was standing to one side, wringing his hands and beseeching the irate firemen, 'Be calm, gentlemen, it's divine to forgive.'

Grave Digger and Coffin Ed were doing their best to stop the fracas.

'Easy does it,' Grave Digger was repeating. Coffin Ed was imploring, 'Let the police have him.' But their pleas had no effect.

A fireman hit the giant across the shins. He went down. Firemen swarmed over him, trying to pin his arms behind him. But the muscles beneath his greasy purpling skin were rock hard. Fingers couldn't get a grip. It was like trying to hold a greased pig at a state fair.

The giant got to his hands and knees and pushed to his feet, shaking off firemen like a dog shedding water. He put his head down and started to run, plowing through a rain of blows.

'The son of a bitch ain't human,' a fireman complained.

He got across the sidewalk and stepped onto the grass. His

foot sunk into the belly of the unconscious dwarf. Globules of vomit spewed from Jake's mouth. No one noticed.

He vaulted over the hood of a fire engine and got a lead on his pursuers.

'Stop him, he's getting away,' a white cop shouted.

Grave Digger and Coffin Ed had moved out into the street, anticipating the breakaway. They had the giant blocked.

The giant drew up as though skidding on his heels. For an instant he stood like a cornered animal, his back to the fire engine, looking for a way out. He had the bruised, bleeding, bewildered look of a bull when the picadors have finished.

'Shall we take him?' Coffin Ed asked.

'Hell, let him go if he can make it,' Grave Digger said.

They drew apart and let the giant through.

Cops and firemen were closing in from both ends of the fire engine. The detectives' car stood obliquely in the street and two prowl cars flanked the other side.

The giant leaped onto the hood of the little black sedan. His rubber-soled sneakers gripped. His next leap took him to the top of a white-and-black prowl car. For a brief instant he was caught in the glare of a fire engine spotlight, a grotesque figure in the strained, shocking, ugly position of panic-stricken flight.

Automatically, as though the target were irresistible, a cop drew a bead with his service revolver. At the same instant, as though part of the same motion sprung from another source, Coffin Ed knocked his arm up with the long nickel-plated barrel of his own revolver. The cop's pistol went off. The giant seemed to fly from the roof of the prowl car and crashed into the foliage of the park.

For a moment everyone was sobered by the sound of the shot and the sight of the giant crashing to earth. All were gripped by the single thought – the cop had shot him. Reactions varied; but all were held in a momentary silence.

Then Coffin Ed said to the cop who had fired the shot, 'You can't kill a man for putting in a false fire alarm.'

The cop had only intended to wing him, but Coffin Ed's rebuke infuriated him.

'Hell, you killed a man for farting at you,' he charged.

Coffin Ed's scarred face twitched in a blind rage. It was the one thing in his career which touched him to the quick.

'That's a goddamned lie!' he shouted, his pistol barrel flashing in a vicious arc toward the white cop's head.

There was just time for Grave Digger to catch the blow in his hand and spin Coffin Ed around.

'Goddammit, Ed, control it, man!' he said. 'It's a joke.'

The white cop was being forcibly held by two of his uniformed mates. 'These two black bastards are crazy,' he mouthed.

Coffin Ed allowed himself to be drawn off by Grave Digger, but he said, 'It ain't no joke to me.'

Grave Digger knew that it was useless to explain that Coffin Ed had shot a different boy, one who was trying to throw perfume into his face. He had thought the boy was throwing acid; and he already bore the scars of one acid bath in his face. Everyone in the department knew the straight story, but some of the white cops distorted it to needle Coffin Ed.

The fracas didn't last more than a minute, but it gave the giant a chance to get away. The park dropped steeply from the manicured fringe bordering Riverside Drive through a rocky jungle of brush down to a wire fence enclosing the tracks of the New York Central Railroad's freight lines and the elevated platform of the six-lane West Side Highway.

A cop heard the giant threshing through the brush and shouted, 'He's making for the river!'

The pursuit commenced again. No one had believed the giant's story of robbery and murder taking place.

'Let 'em go,' Grave Digger said bitterly.

'I ain't stopping 'em,' Coffin Ed said. 'With the start he's got now they won't catch him anyway.'

Grave Digger took off his heavy felt hat and rubbed his palm across his sweat-wet short kinky hair.

They looked at one another with the unspoken communication they had developed during the years they had served as partners.

'You think there's anything in it?' Grave Digger asked.

'We'd better try to find out. It'd be a hell of a note if somebody was being murdered during all this comedy we're having.'

'That would be the story.'

Coffin Ed walked over and looked down at the unconscious dwarf. He bent over and felt his pulse.

'What about our friend Jake?'

'He'll keep,' Grave Digger said. 'Let's go. This halfwit Pinky may be right.'

2

By that time Riverside Drive was wide awake. Vaguely human shapes hung from the dark open windows of the front apartments like an amphitheater of ghosts; and the windows of the back apartments were ablaze with lights as though the next war had begun.

The apartment house they sought was a nine-story brick building with plate-glass doors opening into a dimly lit foyer. The night latch was on. There was a bell to one side above a shiny chrome plate announcing: SUPERINTENDENT. Coffin Ed reached toward it, but Grave Digger shook his head.

Even though the street was packed with fire engines, prowl cars, uniformed cops and firemen, the residents peering from the upper windows watched the two black men suspiciously.

Coffin Ed noticed them and remarked, 'They think we're burglars.'

'Hell, what else they going to think about two spooks like us prowling about in a white neighborhood in the middle of the night?' Grave Digger said cynically. 'If I was to see two white men in Harlem at this time of night I'd figure they were looking for whores.'

'You would be right.'

'No more than them.'

At the side of the building was a narrow cement walk closed

off by a barred iron gate. The gate was locked.

Grave Digger grabbed the top bar with one hand, put a foot on the middle crossbar, and went up and over. Coffin Ed followed.

From somewhere above came the sound of an outraged gasp. They ignored it.

Halfway down the side of the building was a barred window on a level with the sidewalk. Purple light poured out onto the opposite wall in a rectangular bar. They approached it quietly and knelt, one on each side.

The window opened into a room that appeared to have been furnished by the castoffs of decades of tenants. Nothing had escaped. Lowboys and highboys were stacked against the walls, interspersed with marble statuettes, grandfather clocks, iron jockey hitching posts, empty birdcages, a broken glass aquarium, two moth-eaten stuffed squirrels and a molted stuffed owl. On one side was a round-topped dining table, surrounded by a variety of dilapidated chairs, and covered by a faded red silk curtain. Between two doors opening to the kitchen and bedroom respectively stood an old-fashioned organ, atop which was a menagerie of china animals. Opposite were two out-of-date television sets, one atop the other, crowned by a radio from the pre-television age. An overstuffed davenport, flanked by two overstuffed armchairs, was drawn up before the television sets close enough to reach through the screens and manhandle the performers. The linoleum floor was piled with threadbare scatter rugs.

A lamp with a blue bulb burned on a lowboy, vying with a red-bulbed lamp on the dining table. A small fan atop an oak-stained highboy was stirring up the hot air.

The television screens were dark but the radio was playing. It was tuned to a late record program. The voice of Jimmy Rushing issued from the metallic sounding speaker, singing: '*I got that old-fashioned love in my heart . . .*'

A young black man wearing a soiled white turban and a flowing robe of bright-colored rags sat in the center of the davenport, eating a pork chop sandwich and looking over his shoulder with an animated leer.

Behind him a high-yellow woman was doing a chickentail shuffle around the dining table with a dark Jamaica rum highball in one hand. She was wearing a garment that looked like a bleached flour sack with holes cut out for the arms and head. She was a tall, skinny woman with the high sharp hips of a cotton chopper and the big loaded breasts of a wet nurse. As she shuffled barefooted on the pile of rugs, her bony knees poked out the sack in front while her sharp shaking buttocks poked it out in the back like the tail feathers of a laying hen. Up above, her breasts poked out the top of the sack like the snouts of two hungry shoats.

She had a long bony face with a flat nose and jutting chin. Masses of crinkly black hair, dripping with oil, hung down to the middle of her back. Her slanting yellow eyes were doing tricks in the African's direction.

Grave Digger rapped on the window.

The woman gave a start. Liquid sloshed from the glass over the table cover.

The African saw them first. His eyes got white-rimmed.

Then the woman turned and saw them. Her big, wide, cushion-lipped mouth swelled with fury.

'You niggers better get away from that window or I'll call the police,' she shouted in a flat unmusical voice.

Grave Digger fished a felt-lined leather folder from his side coat pocket and showed his buzzer.

The woman went sullen. 'Nigger cops,' she said scornfully. 'What you whore-chasers want?'

'In,' Grave Digger said.

She looked at the drink in her hand as though she didn't know what to do with it. Then she said, 'You cain't come in here. My husband ain't at home.'

'That's all right, you'll do.'

She looked around at the African. He was getting to his feet as though preparing to leave.

'You stay, we want to talk to you too,' Grave Digger said.

The woman jerked her gaze back toward the window. Her eyes were slits of suspicion. 'What you want to talk to him for?'

'Where's the door, woman?' Coffin Ed said sharply. 'Let us ask the questions.'

'It's in the back; where you think it's at?' she said.

They stood up and went around to the back of the building.

'It's been a long time since I've seen a real cat-eyed woman,' Coffin Ed remarked.

'I wouldn't have one for my own for all the tea in China,' Grave Digger declared.

'You just ain't saying it.'

Steps led down to the green-painted basement door. The woman had it open and was waiting for them, arms akimbo.

'Gus ain't in no trouble, is he?' she asked. She didn't look worried; she looked downright evil.

'Who is Gus?' Grave Digger asked, stopping on the bottom.

'He's my husband, the super.'

'What kind of trouble?'

'How would I know? Trouble is your sugar. What would you be doing messing around here at this time of night unless –' She broke off; her slitted yellow eyes became malevolent. 'I just hope ain't none of these grudging-assed white folks has accused us of stealing something, just 'cause we is going to Ghana,' she said in her flat outraged voice. 'It'd be just like 'em.'

'Ghana!' Grave Digger exclaimed. 'Ghana in Africa? You're going to Ghana?'

Her expression became suddenly triumphant. 'You heard me.'

'Who's *we*?' Coffin Ed asked over Grave Digger's shoulder.

'Me and Gus, that's who.'

'Let's go inside and get this straightened out,' Grave Digger said.

'If you think we has stole something, you're beating up the wrong bush,' she said. 'We ain't took nothing from nobody.'

'We'll see.'

She wheeled and went down the brightly lighted, white-washed corridor, her square bony shoulders held high and stiff while her hard sharp buttocks wiggled like a tadpole.

A dark green steamer trunk stood against the wall beside the elevator doors. It bore luggage stickers reading: SS QUEEN MARY – CUNARD LINE – *Hold.*' Both handles were tagged.

The detectives' interest went up another notch.

The door to the janitor's suite opened directly into the over-stuffed parlor. When they entered, the African was sitting on the edge of a straight-backed chair with the rum highball shaking in his hand.

The radio was silent.

As she turned to close the door, an animal appeared silently in the kitchen doorway.

The detectives felt their scalps twitch.

At first sight it appeared to be a female lion. It was tawny-colored with a massive head, upright ears and lambent eyes. Then a low growl issued from its throat and they knew it was a dog.

Coffin Ed slipped his revolver from its holster.

'She won't hurt you,' the woman said scornfully. 'She's chained to the stove.'

'Are you taking this animal with you?' Grave Digger asked in amazement.

'It don't belong to us; it belongs to an albino nigger called Pinky who Gus had around here to help him,' she said.

'Pinky. He's your son, ain't he?' Grave Digger needled.

'My son!' she exploded. 'Do I look like that nigger's ma? He's already older than I is.'

'He calls your husband his father.'

'He ain't no such thing, even if he is old enough. Gus just found him somewhere and took pity on him.'

Coffin Ed nudged Grave Digger to show him four tan plastic suitcases which had been hidden from their view by the dining table.

'So where is Gus?' Grave Digger asked.

She got sullen again. 'I don't know where he's at. Out watching the fire up the street, I suppose.'

'He didn't go out to get a fix, did he?' Grave Digger took a shot in the dark, remembering their prisoner, Jake.

'Gus!' She appeared indignant. 'He ain't got the habit – no kind of habit, unless it's the churchgoing habit.' She thought for a moment and added, 'I guess he must have went to take the trunk from the storage room; I see somebody put it in the hall.'

'Who's got the habit?' Coffin Ed insisted.

'Pinky's got the habit. He's on H.'

'How can he afford it?'

'Don't ask me.'

Grave Digger let his gaze rest on the nervous African.

'What's this man doing here?' he asked her suddenly.

'He's an African chief,' she said proudly.

'I believe you; but that don't answer my question.'

'If you just must know, he sold the farm to Gus.'

'What farm?'

'The cocoa plantation in Ghana where we is going.'

'Your husband bought a cocoa plantation in Ghana from this African?' Coffin Ed said incredulously. 'What kind of racket is this?'

'Show him your passport,' she told the African.

The African fished a passport from the folds of his robe and held it out toward Grave Digger.

Grave Digger ignored it, but Coffin Ed took it and examined it curiously before handing it back.

'I don't dig this,' Grave Digger confessed, removing his hat to scratch his head. 'Where's all this money coming from? Your husband can afford to buy a cocoa plantation in Ghana on a superintendent's salary, and his helper can afford a heroin habit.'

'Don't ask me where Pinky gets his money from,' she said. 'Gus got his on the legit. His wife died and left him a tobacco farm in North Carolina and he sold it.'

Grave Digger and Coffin Ed looked at one another with raised brows.

'I thought you were his wife,' Grave Digger said to the woman.

'I is now,' she said triumphantly.

'Then he's a bigamist.'

She tittered. 'He ain't no more.'

Grave Digger shook his head. 'Some folks have all the luck.'

From outside came the sound of fire engines starting and beginning to move away.

'Where was the fire?' she asked.

'There wasn't any fire,' Grave Digger said. 'It was Pinky who turned in the fire alarm. He wanted to call the police.'

Her slanting yellow eyes stretched into the shape of almonds. 'He did! What did he want to do that for?'

'He said that you and this African were murdering and robbing his father.'

She turned a dirty muddy color. The African jumped to his feet as though he had been stung in the rear by a wasp; he started sputtering denials in a guttural-sounding, strangely accented English. She cut him off harshly, 'Shut up! Gus will take care of him. The dirty mother-raping white nigger! After all we has done for him, trying to make trouble for us on our last day.'

'Why would he do that?'

'He don't like Africans is all. He's just envious 'cause he ain't got no color in his own fishbelly skin.'

Grave Digger and Coffin Ed shook their heads in unison.

'Now I've heard everything,' Grave Digger said. 'Here's a white colored man who puts in a false fire alarm that Riverside Church is on fire, getting half the fire equipment in New York City on the roll and all the police in the neighborhood up here – and why? I ask you why?'

'Because he don't like black colored people,' Coffin Ed said.

'You can't blame that on the heat,' Grave Digger said.

The front doorbell began to ring. It rang long and insistently, as though someone was trying to jab the button through the wall.

'Now who in the hell is that at this hour of the night?' the woman said.

'Maybe it's Gus,' Coffin Ed said. 'Maybe he's lost his key.'

'If Pinky done put in another false fire alarm, he better watch out,' the woman threatened.

She opened the door to the corridor and went to answer the bell. The detectives followed her up the stairs into the front foyer.

Through the glass-paneled doors, uniformed cops were seen swarming about the entrance.

The woman flung open the doors.

'Now what you all want?' she demanded.

The white cops looked suspiciously at the two colored detectives.

'We got several reports that two colored prowlers have been seen around this house,' one of them said in a hard challenging voice. 'You know anything about it?'

'That's us,' Grave Digger said as he and Coffin Ed flashed their buzzers. 'We've been prowling around.'

The white cop reddened.

'Well, don't blame us,' he said. 'We got to check on these reports.'

'Hell, we ain't blaming you,' Grave Digger said. 'It's the heat.'

They left with the other cops and went up the street to look for Jake the dwarf, but he was gone. A prowl car cop still lingering in the vicinity said he had been taken to the hospital.

The fire engines had gone but several deserted prowl cars were still parked haphazardly in the street. Some cops were still searching for Pinky, the giant albino, but they had not found him.

Coffin Ed glanced at his watch.

'It's twelve after two,' he said. 'This joke has lasted for more than an hour.'

'The bars have closed,' Grave Digger said. 'We'd better take a look in the valley before checking in.'

'What about Jake?'

'He'll keep. But first let's look see what's cooking in all this heat.'

They got into their little black sedan and drove off, looking like two farmers who had just arrived in town.

3

It was 3:30 a.m. before they finally got back to the precinct station to write out their report.

The heat had detained them.

Even at past two in the morning, 'The Valley,' that flat lowland of Harlem east of Seventh Avenue, was like the frying pan of hell. Heat was coming out of the pavement, bubbling from the asphalt; and the atmospheric pressure was pushing it back to earth like the lid on a pan.

Colored people were cooking in their overcrowded, overpriced tenements; cooking in the streets, in the after-hours joints, in the brothels; seasoned with vice, disease and crime.

An effluvium of hot stinks arose from the frying pan and hung in the hot motionless air, no higher than the rooftops – the smell of sizzling barbecue, fried hair, exhaust fumes, rotting garbage, cheap perfumes, unwashed bodies, decayed buildings, dog-rat-and-cat offal, whiskey and vomit, and all the old dried-up odors of poverty.

Half-nude people sat in open windows, crowded on the fire escapes, shuffled up and down the sidewalks, prowled up and down the streets in dilapidated cars.

It was too hot to sleep. Everyone was too evil to love. And it was too noisy to relax and dream of cool swimming holes and the shade of chinaberry trees. The night was filled with the blare of countless radios, the frenetic blasting of spasm cats playing in the streets, hysterical laughter, automobile horns, strident curses, loudmouthed arguments, the screams of knife fights.

The bars were closed so they were drinking out of bottles. That was all there was left to do, drink strong bad whiskey and get hotter; and after that steal and fight.

Grave Digger and Coffin Ed had been held up by an outburst of petty crime.

Thieves had broken into a supermarket and had stolen 50 pounds of stew beef, 20 pounds of smoked sausage, 20 pounds of chicken livers, 29 pounds of oleomargarine, 32 pounds of cooking lard, and one TV set.

A drunk had staggered into a funeral parlor and had refused to leave until he got 'first-class service.'

A man had stabbed a woman because she 'wouldn't give him none.'

A woman had stabbed a man whom she claimed had stepped on the corn on her left little toe.

Then on their way in they got held up again by a free-for-all on Eighth Avenue and 126th Street. It had been started by a man attacking another man with a knife in a dice game in a room back of a greasy spoon restaurant. The attacked man had run out into the street and grabbed a piece of iron pipe from a garbage can where he had cached it for just such an emergency before joining the dice game. When the man with the knife saw his erstwhile victim coming back with the iron pipe, he did an about-face and took off in the opposite direction. Then a friend of the man with the knife charged from a dark doorway wielding a baseball bat and began to duel the man with the pipe. The man with the knife turned back to help his friend with the baseball bat. Upon seeing what was happening, the cook came from the greasy spoon, wielding a meat cleaver, and demanded fair play. Whereupon the man with the knife engaged the cook with the cleaver in a separate duel.

When Grave Digger and Coffin Ed arrived at the scene, the hot dusty air was being churned up by the slinging and slashing of weapons.

Without engaging in preliminaries, Coffin Ed began pistol-whipping the man with the knife. The man was staggering about on the sidewalk, holding on to his knife which he was too scared to use; his legs were wobbling and his knees were buckling and he was saying, 'You can't hurt me hitting me on the head.'

With his left hand, Grave Digger began slapping the face of the man with the baseball bat, and with his right hand fanning the air with his pistol to keep back the crowd; at the same time shouting, 'Straighten up!'

Coffin Ed was echoing, 'Count off, red-eye! Fly right!'

Both of them looked just as red-eyed, greasy-faced, sweaty and evil as all the other colored people gathered about, combatants and spectators alike. They were of a similar size and build to other 'working stiffs' – big, broad-shouldered, loose-jointed and flat-footed. Their faces bore marks and scars similar to any colored street fighter. Grave Digger's was full of lumps where felons had hit him from time to time with various weapons; while Coffin Ed's was a patchwork of scars where skin had been grafted over the burns left by acid thrown into his face.

The difference was they had the pistols, and everyone in Harlem knew them as the 'Mens'.

The cook took advantage of this situation to slip back into his kitchen and hide his meat cleaver behind the stove. While the man with the pipe quickly cached his weapon inside his pants leg and went limping rapidly away like a wooden-legged man in a race of one-legged men.

After a little, peace was restored. Without a word or backward glance, Grave Digger and Coffin Ed walked to their car, climbed in and drove off.

They checked into the precinct station and wrote their report.

When Lieutenant Anderson finished reading the statement of the janitor's wife as to the reason Pinky put in the false fire alarm, he asked incredulously, 'Do you believe that?'

'Yeah,' Grave Digger replied. 'I'll believe it until some better reason comes along.'

Lieutenant Anderson shook his head. 'The motives these people have for crimes.'

'When you think about them, they make sense,' Coffin Ed said argumentatively.

Lieutenant Anderson wiped the sweat from his face with a limp dirty handkerchief.

'That's all right for the psychiatrists, but we're cops,' he said.

Grave Digger winked at Coffin Ed.

'If you're white, all right,' he recited in the voice of a schoolboy.

Coffin Ed took it up. *'If you're brown, stick around . . .'*

Grave Digger capped it, *'If you're black, stand back.'*

Lieutenant Anderson reddened. He was accustomed to his two ace detectives needling him, but it always made him feel a little uneasy.

'That might all be true,' he said. 'But these crimes cost the taxpayers money.'

'You ain't kidding,' Grave Digger confirmed.

Coffin Ed changed the subject. 'Have you heard whether they caught him?'

Lieutenant Anderson shook his head. 'They caught everyone but him – bums, perverts, whores, tricks, and one hermit.'

'He won't be too hard to find,' Grave Digger said. 'There ain't too many places for a giant albino Negro turning black-and-blue to hide.'

'All right, let's stop the clowning,' Anderson said. 'What about this charge against a drug pusher?'

'He's one of the big sources of supply for colored addicts up here, but he's smart enough to keep out of Harlem,' Grave Digger said.

'When we saw him choking, we knew he'd been eating the decks he had on him, so before he could digest them we got enough out of him to convict him of possession anyway.'

'It's in that envelope,' Grave Digger said, nodding toward the desk. 'When it's analyzed, they'll find five or six half-chewed decks of heroin.'

Anderson opened the end of the brown manila envelope lying atop the desk which the detectives had turned in as evidence. He shook out the folded handkerchief and opened it.

'Phew!' he exclaimed, drawing back. 'It stinks.'

'It doesn't stink anymore than a dirty pusher,' Grave Digger said. 'I hate this type of criminal worse than God hates sin.'

'What's the other stuff with it?' Anderson asked, pushing the mess about with the tip of his pencil.

Coffin Ed chuckled. 'Whatever he last ate before he started eating evidence.'

Anderson looked sober. 'I know your intentions are good, but you can't go around slugging people in the belly to collect evidence, even if they are felons. You know that this man has been taken to the hospital.'

'Don't worry, he won't protest,' Grave Digger said.

'Not if he knows what's good for him,' Coffin Ed echoed.

'Every precinct's not like Harlem,' Anderson cautioned. 'You get away with tricks here that'll kick back in any other precinct.'

'If this kicks back, I'll eat the foot that did it,' Grave Digger said.

'Talking about eating reminds me that we ain't ate yet,' Coffin Ed said.

Mamie Louise was sick and the other all-night greasy spoons and barbecue joints had no appeal. They decided to eat in the Great Man nightclub on 125th Street.

'I like a joint where you can smell the girls' sweat,' Coffin Ed said.

It had a bar fronting on the street with a cabaret in back where a two-dollar membership fee was charged to get in.

When the detectives flashed their buzzers they were made members for free.

Noise, heat and orgiastic odors hit them as they entered through the curtained doorway. The room was so small and packed that the celebrants rubbed buttocks with others at adjoining tables. Faces bubbled in the dim light like a huge pot of cannibal stew, showing mostly eyes and teeth. Smoke-blackened nudes frolicked in the murals about the fringes of the ceiling. Beneath were pencil sketches of numerous Harlem celebrities, interspersed with autographed photos of jazz greats. A ventilator fan was laboring in the back wall without any noticeable effect.

'You want stink, you got it,' Grave Digger said.

'And everything that goes with it,' Coffin Ed amended.

Some joker was shouting in a loud belligerent voice, 'I ain't gonna pay for but two whiskeys; dat's all I drunk. Somebody musta stole the other three 'cause I ain't seen 'em.'

Behind a dance floor scarcely big enough to hold two pairs of feet, a shining black man wearing a white silk shirt kept banging the same ten keys on a midget piano; while a lank black woman without joints wearing a backless fire-red evening gown did a snake dance about the tables, shouting *Money-money-money-honey*,' and holding up her skirt. She was bare beneath. Whenever someone held out a bill, she changed the lyric to, '*Ohhhweee, daddy, money makes me feel so funny,*' and gave a graphic demonstration by accepting it.

The proprietor cleared a table in the back corner for the two detectives and showed them most of the amalgam fillings in his teeth.

'I believe in live and let live,' he said right off. 'What you gentlemen wish to eat?'

There was a choice of fried chicken, barbecued pork ribs and New Orleans gumbo.

They chose the gumbo, which was the specialty of the house. It was made of fresh pork, chicken gizzards, hog testicles and giant shrimp, with a base of okra and sweet potatoes, and twenty-seven varieties of seasonings, spices and herbs.

'It's guaranteed to cool you off,' the proprietor boasted.

'I don't want to get so cooled off I can't warm up no more,' Grave Digger said.

The proprietor showed him some more teeth in a reassuring smile.

They followed the gumbo with huge quarters of ice-cold watermelon which had black seeds.

While they were eating it, a chorus of four hefty, sepia-colored girls took the floor and began doing a bump dance with their backs to the audience, throwing their big strong smooth-skinned hams about as though juggling hundred-pound sacks of brown sugar.

'Throw it to the wind!' someone shouted.

'Those hams won't stay up on wind,' Coffin Ed muttered.

The tight close air was churned into a steaming bedlam.

The temptation was too great for Coffin Ed. He filled his mouth full of watermelon seeds and began spitting them at the live targets. It was a fifteen-foot shot and before he got the range he had hit a couple of jokers at ringside tables in the back of their necks and almost set off a rumpus. The jokers were puffing up to fight when finally Coffin Ed's shots began landing on the targets. First one girl and then another began leaping and slapping their bottoms as though stung by bees. The audience thought it was part of the act. It was going over big.

One joker was inspired to give an impromptu rendition of 'Ants in your pants.'

Then one of the black seeds stuck to the cream-colored bottom of one of the girls and she captured it. She held it up and looked at it. She stopped dancing and turned an irate face toward the audience.

'Some mother-raper is shooting at me with watermelon seeds,' she declared. 'And I'm gonna find out who it is.'

The other three dancers examined the seed. Then all four of them, looking evil as housemaids scrubbing floors, began pushing between the tables, roughing up the customers, shaking down the joint for someone eating watermelon.

Grave Digger had the presence of mind to whip the plates containing the rinds and seeds from atop the table and hide them on the floor underneath their chairs. No one else was eating watermelon, but Coffin Ed went undiscovered.

When finally the dancing was resumed, Grave Digger let out his breath. 'That was a close shave,' he said.

'Let's get out of here before we get caught,' Coffin Ed said, wiping his mouth with the palm of his hand.

'We! What we?' Grave Digger exploded. The proprietor escorted them to the door. He wouldn't let them pay for the dinners. He gave them a big fat wink, letting them know he was on their side. 'Live and let live, that's my motto,' he said.

'Yeah. Just don't think it buys you anything,' Grave Digger said harshly.

It was pressing 5 a.m. when they came out into the street, almost an hour past their quitting time.

'Let's take a last look for Gus,' Grave Digger suggested.

'What for?' Coffin Ed asked.

'For reference.'

'You don't never give up, do you?' Coffin Ed complained.

It was 5:05 when Grave Digger drove past the apartment over on Riverside Drive. He kept down to Grant's Tomb, turned around and parked on the opposite side of the street, three houses down. Gray dawn was slipping beneath an overcast sky and the sprinklers were already watering the browned grass in the park surrounding the monument.

They were about to alight when they saw the African come from the apartment, leading the mammoth dog by a heavy iron chain. The dog wore an iron-studded muzzle that resembled the visor of a sixteenth-century helmet.

'Sit still,' Grave Digger cautioned.

The African looked up and down the street, then crossed over and walked in the opposite direction. His white turban and many-colored robe looked outlandish against the dull green background of foliage.

'Good thing I'm in New York,' Grave Digger said. 'I'd take him for a Zulu chief out hunting with his pet lion.'

'Better follow him, eh?' Coffin Ed said.

'To watch the dog piss?'

'It was your idea.'

The African turned down steps descending into the park and passed out of sight.

They sat watching the apartment entrance. Minutes passed. Finally Coffin Ed suggested, 'Maybe we'd better buzz her; see what's cooking.'

'Hell, if Gus ain't there, all we'll find is dirty sheets,' Grave

Digger said. 'And if he's home he's going to want to know what we're doing busting into his house when we're off duty.'

'Then what the hell did we come for?' Coffin Ed flared.

'It was just a hunch,' Grave Digger admitted.

They lapsed into silence.

The African ascended the stairs from the park.

Coffin Ed looked at his watch. It read 5:27.

The African was alone.

They watched him curiously as he crossed the street and pressed the bell to the apartment. They saw him turn the knob and go inside. They looked at one another.

'Now what the hell does that mean?' Coffin Ed said.

'Means he got rid of the dog.'

'What for?'

'The question is, how?' Grave Digger amended.

'Well, don't ask me. I'm no Ouija board.'

'Hell with this, let's go home,' Grave Digger decided suddenly.

'Don't growl at me, man, you're the one who suggested this nonsense.'

4

Pinky peered through the plate-glass window of a laundrymat at the corner of 225th Street and White Plains Road in the Bronx. There was an electric clock on the back wall. The time read 3:33.

The sky was overcast with heavy black clouds. The hot sultry air was oppressive, as before a thunderstorm. The elevated trestle of the IRT subway line loomed overhead, eerie and silent, snaking down the curve of White Plains Road. As far as he could see, the streets were empty of life. The silence was unreal.

He reckoned it had taken him more than an hour to get there from the Riverside Park in Manhattan. He had covered part of the distance by hopping a New York Central switch engine, but afterwards he had slunk along endless blocks of silent, sleeping residential streets, ducking to cover when anyone hove into view.

Now he began to feel safe. But his body was still trembling as though he had the ague.

He turned east in the direction of the Italian section.

Apartment buildings gave way to pastel-colored villas of southern Italian architecture, garnished with flower gardens and plaster saints. After a while the houses became scattered, interspersed by market gardens and vacant lots overgrown with weeds in which hoboes slept and goats were tethered.

Finally he reached his destination, a weather-stained, one-storied, pink stucco villa at the end of an unfinished street without sidewalks. It was a small house flanked by vacant lots used for rubbish dumps. Oddly enough, it had a large gabled attic. It sat far back of a wire fence enclosing a front yard of burnt grass, dried-up flowers and wildly thriving weeds. In a niche over the front door was a white-marble crucifix of a singularly lean and tortured Christ, encrusted with bird droppings. In other niches at intervals beneath the eaves were all the varicolored plaster saints good to the souls of Italian peasants.

All of the front windows were closed and shuttered. Save for the faint sounds of a heavy boogie beat on a piano, the house seemed abandoned.

Pinky vaulted the fence and followed a path through tall weeds around the side of the house, taking care to avoid a concrete birdbath, an iron statue of Garibaldi and a large zinc vase of artificial roses.

There was a deep backyard enclosed by a high plank fence. The back door opened onto a grape arbor with thick clusters of purple grapes hanging between the dusty leaves. To one side was a rotting tool-and-wood shed adjoining a chicken coop and rabbit hutch. From the door of the tool shed a tethered nanny goat gazed at Pinky from sad wise eyes. Beyond was a dusty vegetable garden dying from thirst and neglect. But along the back fence a patch of well-watered, carefully tended marijuana weeds grew adjacent to a garage of corrugated steel.

Pinky halted in the dark beside the arbor and listened. He breathed in a choking manner and tears streamed down his cheeks.

Now the sound of music was loud and defiant. Vying with the hard banging of piano notes was the ratchetlike rhythm of someone strumming an accompaniment on a double-sided wooden washboard. It sounded like a cross between bone-beating and rim-rapping.

The two attic windows were wide open. Through the left-side one, from where he stood, Pinky saw the back of an upright piano, atop which sat a kerosene lamp and a half-filled bottle of gin. As he watched, a black, pudgy-fingered hand rose from the far side of the piano and grasped the gin bottle. The tempo of the piano changed. Instead of two-handed playing with the steady bass beat marching alongside the light fantastic tripping on the treble keys, there followed a wild left-hand riffing the whole length of the board.

The hand holding the bottle reappeared. The hand withdrew. The bottle remained. The level of the gin had lowered noticeably. Suddenly the bass came in again like John Henry driving steel and the treble notes ran through the night like the patter of rain.

Then another black hand appeared from the other side of the piano and took down the bottle. The sound of rim-rapping ceased and only the sound of beating bones continued. One side of the washboard had conked out. The hand and the bottle reappeared. After which the rapping went wild.

Through the right-side window could be seen vague figures of shirt-sleeved men and black-shouldered women swaying back and forth, locked in tight embrace; the locked liquid motions steady and unchanging despite the eccentricity of the music, sometimes keeping on the beats, sometimes in between. The Bear Hug and the Georgia Grind were being performed with a slow steady motion. Black skin gleamed like oily shadows in the dim yellow rays of the single flickering light of the kerosene lamp.

'Missa Pinky,' came a soft small voice from the dark.

Pinky jumped and wheeled about.

Big white circles shone from a small black face almost invisible in the dark. The skinny barefooted figure was clad in a patched mansize overall jumper.

'Boy, what you want at this time of night?' Pinky said roughly.

'Will you please, sir, go up and ask Sister Heavenly for two pods of Heavenly Dust for Uncle Bud?'

'Why don't you go up and get it yourself?'

'She won't sell it to me. I is too young.'

'Why don't Uncle Bud come get it hisself?'

'He's feeling po'ly. That's why he sent me. He ain't got the faith no more.'

'All right, give me the money.'

The boy stuck out a hand holding two crumpled dollar bills. Pinky went beneath the arbor and knocked on the back door.

'Who dat?' a disembodied voice asked from within.

'Me, Pinky.'

Two white crescents flickered briefly in a glass pane of the upper-door panel. There was the click of a simple mortise lock and the door swung open.

With his eyes accustomed to the dark, Pinky made out the vague figure of a stone-old, gray-haired man clad in a blue cotton nightgown which seemed to float about the pitch-dark kitchen. Faint bluish gleams came from a double-barreled shotgun which the old man held cradled in his right arm.

'How is you, Uncle Saint?' Pinky greeted politely.

'Middling,' the old man replied. His voice seemed to come from another part of the room.

'I's going up to see Sister Heavenly.'

'You got feet, ain't you?' Now his voice seemed to come out of the floorboards between Pinky's feet.

Pinky grinned dutifully and went through the kitchen toward the stairs in the back hall.

He found Sister Heavenly sitting on a high throne chair in the corner of the attic farthest from the light. In the dark shadows she was an indistinguishable shape wrapped in dull black cloth.

A sick man lay on a stretcher on the floor at her feet.

Sister Heavenly was a faith healer. Pinky didn't dare approach her while she was 'ministering.'

'You is going to be happy,' she crooned in an old, cracked voice which still retained remnants of a bygone music. 'You is going to be happy – if you got the faith.'

Her body swayed from side to side in time with the slow steady beat of the bass.

The man on the stretcher said in a weak voice, 'I is got the faith.'

She crept down from the throne and knelt by his side.

Her thin, clawlike, transparent hand extended a silver spoon containing white powder toward his face.

'Inhale,' she said. 'Inhale deeply. Breathe the Heavenly Dust into your heart.'

The man sniffed rapidly four times in succession, each stronger than the previous.

She climbed back into her throne.

'Now you is going to be healed,' she crooned.

Pinky waited patiently until she deigned to see him. She forbade interruptions.

Sister Heavenly prided herself on being an old-fashioned faith healer with old-fashioned tried-and-true methods. That was why she used old-fashioned gin-drinking musicians and directed her clients to dance old-fashioned belly-rubbing dances. It was the first stage of the cure. She called it 'de-incarnation.'

She had kept Black Key Shorty on the piano for fifteen years. Washboard Wharton had come later. Both were relics of a bygone time. Washboard sat beside the piano holding a double-sided washboard which he strummed with rabbit-leg bones between his legs. Black Key had learned to play the piano in flats. Both were gin drinkers. They were the only ones she permitted to drink gin in her 'Heavenly Clinic.' There was nothing wrong with them. But she had to heal the sick people who came to her with Heavenly Dust.

'What you want, Pinky?' she asked suddenly.

He gave a start; he didn't think she had seen him.

'You got to help me, Sister Heavenly, I is in trouble,' he blurted out.

She looked at him. 'You've been beat up.'

'How can you tell that, in all this dark?'

'You don't have no milk shine like you generally does.' On second thought she added sharply, 'If it's the police who done it, you git away from here. I don't want no truck with the police.'

'It weren't the police,' he said evasively.

'Well, then you tell me about it later. I ain't got no time to listen to it now.'

'It ain't only that,' he said. 'There's a little tadpole down in the backyard wants two pods of Heavenly Dust for Uncle Bud.'

'I ain't selling no pods to little punks,' she snapped.

'It ain't for him, it's for Uncle Bud; and you don't have to give it to him, I'll do that,' he said.

'Well, give me the money,' she said impatiently.

He handed her the two crumpled dollar bills.

She examined the money with disgust. 'I ain't selling no pods for a dollar no more. Leastways not at this time of night.' She took one small paper packet from somewhere beneath her layers of garments and handed it to him. 'You give him this and tell him the price is two dollars,' she directed, grumbling to herself. 'How do them cheapskates expect to get healed for a dollar, with prices of everything as high as they is?'

'Another thing,' he said hesitantly. 'I need a fix bad.'

'Go see your friend,' she said shortly. 'He'll stake you to a fix.'

'He ain't my friend no more. He's in jail.'

She wheeled about on her throne. 'Don't tell me you were in the rumble with him, 'cause if you've come here with yourself all hot, I'll turn you in myself.'

'I weren't with Jake when they caught him,' he denied evasively.

She was staring at him sharply as though she could see in the dark.

'Well, go down and open the buck rabbit and take a pill out,' she relented. 'And don't take but one, it's all you'll need, it's a speedball. And be sure to close him up good. The spike's in my bureau drawer.'

As he started to turn away, she added, 'And don't think you're putting nothing over on me 'cause I ain't through with you yet. You just wait until I get time to talk to you.'

'I got to talk to you too,' he said.

The man on the stretcher was twitching in time to the music. 'It's cool, Sister Heavenly,' he said in the voice of a convert giving a testimonial. 'I got the real cool faith.'

Black Key Shorty was driving piles on the bass with his steady left hand while his right hand was frolicking over hot dry grass in a nudist's colony. Washboard Wharton was giving out with grunting sounds like a boar hog in a pen full of sows.

The strong orgiastic smell of sweat and red-hot glands was pouring from the windows into the hot sultry air.

It didn't mean a thing to Pinky. He felt so much like crying he was thinking only of a fix. He went down the stairs to the hallway and passed through the kitchen.

Uncle Saint floated from the shadows with his double-barreled shotgun.

'I'll be right back,' Pinky said. 'Sister Heavenly sent me to tap the rabbit.'

'Don't tell me your troubles, I ain't your pappy,' Uncle Saint said, unlocking the door. His voice sounded as though it had come from the bottom of a well.

The little boy in the overall jumper was waiting for Pinky in the grape arbor. He had discovered the grapes but was scared to take any.

'Did you get 'em, Missa Pinky?' he asked timidly.

Pinky fished the packet from his pocket. 'Here, you give this to Uncle Bud and tell 'im the price has gone up. Tell him Sister Heavenly say don't expect to get healed for nothing.'

Reluctantly the little boy accepted the single pod. He knew he'd get a beating for bringing back only one. But there wasn't anything to do about it.

'Yessa,' he said and went slowly into the shadows.

Pinky went to the rabbit hutch, reached through the hatch and caught the buck by the ears. With a deft motion of his free hand, he removed a small square of adhesive tape covering the rabbit's rectum, then withdrew a long rubber plug with a tiny metal handle like a sink stopper. The rabbit remained motionless, staring at him from enormous fear-frozen eyes. He squeezed the rabbit's stomach and a small aluminum capsule popped out. He put the capsule into his pants pocket and restoppered the rabbit.

He wondered what other hiding places Sister Heavenly had. He was her nephew and her only living relative, but she had never told him anything. He reckoned she was getting ready to eat the rabbit if she let him know that much.

At the kitchen door he again went through the amenities with Uncle Saint.

'I'm going to Sister Heavenly's room for a bang.'

'You must think I'm the recording angel,' Uncle Saint grumbled. His voice sounded as though it came out of the oven. 'Go to the devil, for all I care.'

Pinky knew this wasn't true, but he didn't challenge it. He

knew that Uncle Saint would curse up a fit if he went somewhere in the house without telling him in advance.

The top bureau drawer looked like the last stand of a hypochondriac. He found the hypodermic needle lying in the midst of syringes, thermometers, hatpins and hairpins, tweezers, shoe buttoners, and old-fashioned glass-topped bottles containing enough varicolored poisons to decimate an entire narcotics squad. The alcohol lamp sat openly on a marble-topped table in the corner, alongside a battered teapot and a set of stained test tubes. The sugar spoon was in a sugar bowl on the night table beside the bed.

He lit the lamp and sterilized the needle over the flame. Then he emptied the white powdered cocaine and heroin from the aluminum capsule into the sugar spoon and melted it over the flame. He drew the liquid through the needle into the syringe and, holding the spike in his right hand, banged himself in the vein of his left arm while the C & H was still warm.

'Ahhh,' he said softly as the drug went in.

Afterwards he put out the lamp and returned the spike to the medicine drawer.

The speedball had immediate effect. He went back to the kitchen stepping on air.

He knew Sister Heavenly wouldn't be ready for him yet, so he passed the time with the ancient gunman.

'How long is you been a ventriloquist, Uncle Saint?'

'Boy, I been throwing my voice so long, I don't know where it's at anymore myself,' Uncle Saint said. His voice seemed to come from the bedroom Pinky had just quit. Abruptly he laughed at his own joke, 'Ha-ha-ha.' The laughter seemed to come from outside the back door.

'You're going to keep on throwing it around until it gets away some day,' Pinky said.

'What business is it of yours? Is you my keeper?' Uncle Saint crabbed. He sounded like a ghost lurking underneath the floor.

Upstairs, Black Key Shorty was riffing with his left hand again. Pinky knew that the gin bottle was pressed to his lips. Washboard Wharton was making like a skeleton with the galloping itch, waiting his turn.

Pinky listened to the steady clumping of feet on the wooden floor. Everything was crystal clear to him again. He knew just what he had to do. But it was getting late.

5

The pilgrims had finally gone.

Sister Heavenly was sitting up in bed, wearing a pink crocheted bed jacket trimmed in frilly lace. Long, curly, midnight-blue hair of a wig hung down over her shoulders.

She was so old her face had the shrunken, dried-up leathery look of a monkey's. The corneas of her eyes were a strange shade of glazed blue resembling an enameled surface, while the pupils were a faded ocher with white spots. She wore perfect-fitting plates of brilliant, matched, incredibly white teeth.

As a young woman her skin had been black; but daily applications of bleach creams for more than half a century had lightened her complexion to the color of pigskin. Her toothpick arms, extending from the pink jacket, were purple-hued at the top, graduating to parchment-colored hands so thin and fragile-looking as to appear transparent.

In one hand she held a scalding hot cup of sassafras tea, with her little finger extended according to the dictates of etiquette; in the other a small, dainty, meerschaum pipe with a long curved stem and a carved bowl. She was smoking the finely ground stems of marijuana leaves, her only vice.

Pinky sat beside the bed on a green leather ottoman, wringing his ham-size, milk-white hands.

The only light in the room came from a pink-shaded light on

the other side of the bed. The soft pink light gave Pinky's bruised white skin the exotic coloring of some unknown tropical sea monster.

'How come you think they's going to croak him?' Sister Heavenly asked in her deep, slightly cracked, musical voice.

'To rob him, that's why,' Pinky said in his whining voice. 'To get his farm in Ghana.'

'A farm in Ghana!' she said scornfully. 'If Gus got a farm in Ghana I got a palace in heaven.'

'He got a farm, all right. I has seen the papers.'

'Taking he got a farm – which he ain't – how they going to get it by croaking him?'

'She's his wife. He done willed it to her.'

'His wife! She ain't no more his wife than you is his son. If they croak him, it'll go to his relatives – if he got any relatives.'

'She his wife all right. I has seen the license.'

'You has seen everything. Suppose they croak him. They can't go live on his farm. That's the first place the police will look.'

He realized she wasn't convinced about the farm. He took another tack.

'Then it's his money. They'll get that and run away.'

'His money! I is too old and time is too short for this bullshit. Gus ain't never had two white quarters to rub together in his life.'

'He got money. A whole lot of money.' He looked away evasively and his voice changed. 'His other wife in Fayetteville, North Carolina, died and left him a big tobacco farm and he sold it for a heap of money.'

She took a long puff from her pipe and held it down by sipping tea. Her old faded eyes regarded him with cynical amusement over the rim of her cup. Finally, when she let the smoke dribble from her lungs, she said, 'What you trying to con me out of?'

'I ain't trying to con you.'

'Then what's all this 'bout his other wife and his other farm, an' all his money? You must be seeing double.'

'It's the God's truth,' he said, avoiding her eyes. 'I swear it.'

'You swear it. Long as I knowed Gus he ain't never let no woman get no legal hold on him. And if you think any woman what knows that is fool enough to die and leave him something, you don't know the female race.'

'He got something,' he maintained urgently. 'He made me promise not to tell, but I knows it's what they's after.'

She smiled evilly. 'Then why don't you get it yourself, if it's worth anything – poor as you is?' Her voice dripped sarcasm.

'I couldn't rob Gus. He the only one who ever been good to me.'

'You get it and let them rob and murder you, if you is so set on protecting him.'

His face took on a desperate expression. Sweat trickled from the borders of his hair. Tears welled up in his eyes.

'You sitting there, making fun, and he might be dead,' he accused in his whining voice.

Slowly she put down her cup on the night table. She rested the pipe across her stomach and studied him deliberately. She saw that something was troubling him. She realized with faint surprise that he was deadly earnest.

'Ain't I been good to you, too, treating you like my own son – if I had a son?' she cajoled.

'Yassum,' he replied obediently. 'But he took me in and called me his son.'

'Ain't I told you time and again that you is my heir?' she insisted. 'Ain't I told you that you is going to inherit all that I got when I die?'

'Yassum, but you ain't helping me now.'

'You ain't got no right to hold out on me like this. God won't like it,' she said.

'I ain't holding out,' he whined, looking trapped. 'It's just that I promised not to tell.'

She leaned forward and held his eyes in a hypnotic stare. 'Is it in a trunk?'

Her eyes were like two balls of colored fire bearing down on him.

'Not when I seen it.'

'Is it in a sack?'

He felt his power to defy her slipping away.

'Twarn't in no sack when I seen it.'

'Were it hidden in the house?'

He shook his head.

'In the closet? . . . Beneath the floor? . . . Behind the wall?'

He felt himself growing dizzy in a holocaust of lights.

'That ain't how it were hidden,' he admitted.

'He got it on him,' she said triumphantly.

He was too worn out by her eyes to resist further.

'Yassum. In a money belt.'

Intense thought wrinkled her face like a prune. 'It's jewelry,' she concluded. 'He's stolen some jewelry. Is it diamonds?'

His willpower gave way. He slumped forward and sighed. 'It's a treasure map,' he confessed. 'It tells how to find a whole mess of buried treasure in Africa.'

Her eyes popped open as though the lids had broken.

'Treasure map!' she screamed. 'Lost treasure! You still believe in lost treasure, as old as you is?'

'I know how it sound, but that's what it is all right,' he maintained stubbornly.

She stared at him speculatively until he felt himself withering.

'Did you see it?' she asked finally.

'Yassum. It shows a river and the sea and just where the treasure is buried on the bank.'

'A river!' Her eyes glittered as her brain worked lightning fast. 'Where did he get it?'

'He's had it.'

Her eyes narrowed. 'When he show it to you?'

He hesitated before answering. 'Last night.'

'Don't nobody but you know he got it?'

'His wife and the African know. He's going to give it to the expressmen who come for his trunk this morning. They're going to send it on to his farm in Ghana so can't nobody rob him of it before he gets there. But I knows that woman and the African plan to kill him and take it before the expressmen get there – if they ain't already done it.'

'Why didn't you stay with him and protect him?'

'He wouldn't let me; he said he had something to do. He went off and I didn't know where he was at. That's why I rung the fire alarm.'

'What time are the expressmen due?'

'Six o'clock.'

She drew from inside her gown an old-fashioned locket-watch attached to a thin gold chain. It read 5:27.

She jumped out of bed and began to dress. First she snatched off the black wig and substituted a gray one.

'You'll find some green stuff in a bottle in the drawer,' she said. 'Give yourself a shot. It'll calm you. You're too jumpy with all that C.'

While he was loading the spike and banging himself, she dressed rapidly. She paid him no attention.

She put on a flowing black gown over numerous petticoats, low-heeled black shoes and black silk gloves, elbow length. She pinned a small black straw hat to her gray wig with a long steel hatpin.

'Go start the car,' she said.

She listened until he had gone out of the back door. Then she picked up a large black-beaded handbag, got a black-and-white striped parasol from the closet, and went into the kitchen.

Uncle Saint had already dressed. He now wore a black chauffeur's uniform and cap, several sizes too large for him, and of a fashion popular during the 1920s.

'Did you get it?' she asked tersely.

'I heered him,' he replied straight from his mouth. 'If Gus's cut is big enough to buy a farm, it can't be chicken feed – whatever it is.'

'I have an idea what it is,' she said. 'If we ain't too late.'

'Let's go then.'

She went outside. He picked up his shotgun from beside the doorway and followed her, closing and locking the door behind him. He was high as a kite.

Although objects were already visible in the gray dawn light, they did not see Pinky. But they heard him. He was on his knees on the hard-packed dirt floor of the garage, gripping the doorposts with his hands, trying to get to his feet, breathing in loud hard gasps. The muscles of his neck, arms and torso were corded; his blood vessels stood out like ropes.

'He's got the constitution of an ox,' Uncle Saint said.

'*Shhh*,' Sister Heavenly cautioned. 'He can still hear.'

His sense of hearing was unbearably heightened, and he heard every word they said as distinctly as though they had shouted. His mind was lucid. She gave me a knockout drop, he was thinking. But he could feel consciousness leaving him like a wrecked ship sinking slowly into the sea. Finally his muscles collapsed and he went down onto his face between the doorposts. He didn't hear Sister Heavenly and Uncle Saint when they approached.

Uncle Saint reached inside the garage and turned on the light. A 1937 black Lincoln Continental sprang into view.

They stepped over Pinky without comment and left him lying there. Sister Heavenly got into the back. Uncle Saint placed the shotgun within easy reach on the floor of the front seat, then went forward to open the double doors.

He followed a dirt road across an abandoned field, pushing up to fifty, bouncing over rocks and ruts, leaving a cloud of dust. A gardener in his undershirt, wearing a straw hat, was milking a goat tethered to a tree. He paid no attention to the black limousine; it was a common sight. But when Uncle Saint got onto the macadam streets and pushed up to seventy and seventy-five, early-morning workers, milkmen and garbage collectors, turned to stare.

6

Uncle Saint sat in the Lincoln and watched the entrance to the apartment. It was parked in the same place Grave Digger and Coffin Ed had vacated less than an hour earlier.

Sister Heavenly had gone inside to look for Gus. But Uncle Saint didn't take any stock in Pinky's story about a map. The way he figured, Gus was a connection for racketeers smuggling diamonds or maybe gold. He was picking it up somewhere and passing it on.

Sister Heavenly reckoned that Gus was carrying the boodle on him. But Uncle Saint didn't figure it that way. Whatever it was would be in the trunk, he decided. You had to figure that racketeers who would use an old square like Gus for a connection knew what they were doing. And a trunk was still the best means of smuggling anything hot – because it was so obvious. All the smart federal men and slick city dicks would figure racketeers too smart to use an old worn-out gimmick like a trunk. And that was where the racketeers could outsmart them. Just plain human nature. Like the best mark is the one who has been clipped before; he figures then that he knows everything.

As he sat there and turned it over in his mind, Uncle Saint resolved to get that trunk for himself.

For more than twenty-five years he had flunkied for Sister Heavenly, serving her as guard, cook, nurse and toady – doing her dirty work. Before that he had been her lover. But when she had thrown him over, he had hung around like a homeless dog through a long succession of subsequent lovers. Now all he had for her was hate, but he couldn't leave her because he didn't have anywhere else to go, and she knew it.

So he decided to cross her, get the boodle and cut out. Leave her taking the rap. See how she'd handle a mob of racketeers.

He saw a green panel truck pull up before the apartment house entrance. It looked similar to a Railway Express Company truck except for the name in white letters on its side: ACME EXPRESS CO.

Two white men in hickory-striped uniforms and blue-visored caps got out. One was tall and thin, the other medium height and heavyset. Both were clean-shaven and neither wore glasses. That was all Uncle Saint noticed.

Both men glanced toward the Lincoln. It was the only parked car with an occupant. But sight of the old liveried colored pappy behind the wheel allayed their suspicions.

Uncle Saint had a sour grin as they turned their backs and walked toward the door. They had him cased as a square like old Gus, he figured. On the one hand it rankled; but on the other it worked in his favor.

He waited until they had gone inside, then started the motor and kept it idling. He figured he was going to have to hijack the trunk. But not here in front of the apartment house. It was too open and there was no telling what Nosy Parker might be watching him from behind some curtained window, wondering what a strange limousine was doing in the neighborhood at this hour of morning. He just hoped Sister Heavenly wouldn't do anything to rank his play.

Sister Heavenly was sitting in the janitor's parlor, covering the janitor's wife and the African with a blunt-nosed .38-caliber revolver, when the doorbell rang.

'I got to go and open the front door,' the janitor's wife said. 'It's most likely Gus.'

She was standing beside the African, who was seated before the table, where she had backed when Sister Heavenly got the drop on her.

'Can the bullshit and press the buzzer,' Sister Heavenly said, motioning with the barrel of the pistol from where she sat on the arm of the davenport. 'When they get here we'll see who it is.'

The janitor's wife shuffled sullenly over toward the door and pressed a button releasing the latch on the entrance door. She was barefooted and still wore the same cotton shift as before, but now it looked as though she had been rolling in it. Her face was greasy and her slanting yellow eyes glittered evilly.

'You ain't going to get nothing by this, whatever it is you is after,' she muttered in her gravelly voice.

'Just get back over there and shut up,' Sister Heavenly said with an arrogant wave of the gun barrel.

The janitor's wife shuffled back to the side of the African.

The African sat with drooping body, like a melted statue, his white-rimmed eyes staring at the pistol as though hypnotized.

They waited. Only their heavy breathing was audible in the surrounding silence.

The two expressmen saw the trunk in the basement corridor beside the elevator and took it away without seeing anyone.

Uncle Saint was watching when they returned to the street, carrying a large green steamer trunk, stickered and tagged for shipping. They put the trunk into the body of the truck, closed the doors, and looked once again toward the parked Lincoln.

Without appearing to notice them, Uncle Saint leaned out the car window and looked up toward the front windows of the third-story apartment as though listening to someone speaking to him.

The expressmen looked in the same direction, but they didn't see anything.

'Yassum,' Uncle Saint called in a flunkey's voice. 'Right away, mum.'

He put the Lincoln in gear and drove past the express truck without giving it a look and kept on down Riverside Drive, keeping within the twenty-five-mile speed limit.

The expressmen got into the compartment of the truck. The driver started the motor and the truck took off behind the limousine at a more rapid speed.

Uncle Saint accelerated, watching the following truck in his rearview mirror. He kept well ahead, lengthening and shortening the gap between as though driving naturally.

He knew he was playing a dangerous game, especially alone. But he was too old and had lived too long on the edge of violence to be scared of death. What scared him was the idea of what he planned to do. What was in his favor was the fact nobody knew him. No one but Pinky and Sister Heavenly knew his straight monicker; in recent years but few people had seen him in the light. If he could get it and get away, only those two would know who had done it, and even they wouldn't know where to look for him.

He accelerated gradually as he realized the truck was headed downtown, and pulled far ahead. He was two blocks ahead on the almost empty drive when he came to the entrance to the Yacht Club at 79th Street. He swerved into the curving driveway and slowed down, hidden by the dense foliage of the crescent-shaped park. He got a glimpse of the truck passing on Riverside Drive. He came back into the drive a block behind it and kept a bakery truck in between down as far as 72nd Street.

The truck turned east on 72nd Street to Tenth Avenue, and went south. It was a southbound avenue, feeding the Lincoln and Holland tunnels underneath the Hudson River, and was fairly covered with commercial traffic at this hour. That made it easy. The express truck had only one rearview mirror on the left front fender. Uncle Saint kept far to the right, and always kept some vehicle in between.

At 56th Street when the truck turned toward the Hudson River the Lincoln was exposed for a moment or two; but when the truck turned south again alongside the overhead trestle of the New York Central Railroad line, he was covered again. On the west side of the wide brick-paved avenue, the whole length of North River was closed in by the docks of the great oceangoing lines. Underneath the trestle, as far as the eye could see, trucks and truck-trailers were parked side by side. The southbound lane was heavy with traffic feeding the docks.

Already the funnels of the *Queen Mary* at dock could be seen overtopping the wharf of the French Line adjoining the Cunard pier. The express truck swerved toward the curb and braked to a sudden stop behind a black Buick sedan parked less than fifty yards from the entrance to the French Line dock.

The maneuver was executed so quickly Uncle Saint didn't have a chance to stop behind the truck and had to pull ahead of the Buick to park.

It was a no-parking zone and two cops in a prowl car looked meaningfully at the three parked vehicles as they drove slowly by. Being as one was a chauffeur-driven limousine and another an express truck, the cops let them slide for a moment.

Two dark-suited, straw-hatted, somber-looking men sat in the front seat of the Buick and watched the prowl car pass the Cunard dock and drop out of sight in the traffic. The man on the curb side opened the door and stepped out onto the sidewalk. He was a heavyset, black-haired man with a thick-featured, olive-skinned face and a bulging belly. His black single-breasted coat was buttoned at the bottom. He came down the street, looking anxiously toward the exit of the French Line wharf.

Uncle Saint watched in the rearview mirror, concentrating on the men in the express truck.

The driver of the Buick sat with his right hand on the wheel, his left hanging loosely through the open window.

When the heavyset man came level with the curb-side window of the Lincoln, he turned with a quick, catlike motion, unexpected in a man of his build, and came toward the car. He clapped his left hand on the car top, flipped open his coat and drew from a left shoulder sling. When he bent over to peer through the window, as though speaking to the gray-haired old chauffeur, his flapping coat shielded the pistol from view. It was a single-shot derringer with a six-inch perforated silencer attached. Without speaking a word, he took careful aim at the softest spot in Uncle Saint's head. His dull dark eyes were impassive.

Abruptly from behind him a hard voice shouted, 'Get 'em up or I'll shoot!'

He didn't see the faint motion of Uncle Saint's lips. He wheeled about convulsively, the back of his head striking the top of the doorframe, knocking off his hat onto the seat of the car.

Uncle Saint lunged for his shotgun lying on the floor.

The gunman wheeled back, his eyes bugging out, as Uncle Saint was bringing up the muzzle of the double-barreled shotgun.

Both fired simultaneously.

The small coughing sound of the silenced derringer was lost in the heavy booming blast of the shotgun.

In his panic, Uncle Saint had squeezed the triggers of both barrels.

The gunman's face disappeared and his thick heavy body was

knocked over backward from the impact of the 12-gauge shells.

The rear light of a truck parked beneath the trestle in the middle of the avenue disintegrated for no apparent reason.

The air stunk with the smell of cordite and burnt flesh as the driver of the Buick leaned out the window and emptied an automatic pistol held in his left hand.

Holes popped into the back of the Lincoln's tonneau and the left-side rearview mirror was shattered.

Uncle Saint hadn't been touched, but his nappy hair was standing up like iron filings beneath a magnet.

Abruptly a woman began to scream in high, piercing, repetitious shrieks.

Uncle Saint felt as though the top of his head was coming off.

Then men began to shout; horns blew; a police whistle shrilled, and there was a sudden shower of running feet.

Both cars took off at once.

A trailer truck was passing on the left side and a taxi coming from the French Line dock blocked the traffic lane ahead. Porters and stevedores were running up the sidewalk and a uniformed cop with a pistol in his hand was trying to break through.

Uncle Saint was looking through a blind haze of panic. His brain had stopped working. He was driving instinctively, like a fox encircled by hounds.

The truck was to his left, the taxi was in front; he pulled to the right, up over the curb, heading behind the taxi. The running men scattered, diving for safety, as the two cars roared down the broad sidewalk, the Buick following the Lincoln bumper to bumper.

At the entrance to the dock a porter was loading luggage from a taxi onto a four-wheeled cart. He didn't see the Lincoln until it hit the cart. He sailed into the air, clinging to the suitcase as though running to catch a train waiting somewhere in the sky, while other luggage flew past like startled birds. The cart raced down the pier and dove into the sea. The porter came down feetfirst on top of the following Buick, did a perfect somersault and landed sitting on the suitcase his astounded black face an ellipsoid of white eyeballs and white teeth.

In front of the Cunard Line dock Uncle Saint found an opening back to the street. He turned into it but couldn't straighten out fast enough and crossed in front of the same trailer truck he had already passed on the sidewalk. It was so close the truck bumper passed overtop and left rear fender of the Lincoln as he barely missed the concrete pier of the railroad trestle on the other side.

Rubber screamed on the dry brick pavement as the truck driver applied air brakes. The truck horn bleated desperately. But it didn't save the Buick following in the wake of the Lincoln. The truck hit it broadside. The sound of metal rending metal shattered the din. A senseless pandemonium broke out up and down the street.

The truck had overturned the Buick and the front wheels had run overtop it. Hundreds of people were running in all directions without rhyme or reason.

Uncle Saint got away.

He didn't see the accident or hear the sound. He was on the inside traffic lane and it was clear for nine straight blocks. Instinctively he looked into the rearview mirror. Behind him the avenue was empty.

Traffic had been stopped at the scene of the accident. The first two prowl cars to arrive had blocked off the street. For the moment the black Lincoln had been forgotten. By the time the cops got around to gathering evidence, Uncle Saint had passed 42nd Street. None of the witnesses had recognized the make of the car; no one had thought to take the license number; all descriptions of the driver were conflicting.

Suddenly Uncle Saint found himself caught in one of the clover-leaf approaches to the Lincoln Tunnel. The three traffic lanes were jammed with vehicles, bumper to bumper. There was no turning back.

As he crawled along in back of a refrigerator truck, his panic cooled to a sardonic, inverted scare. The killing didn't bother him whatever. 'Thought the old darky was tame,' he muttered to himself.

A subtle change came over him. He reverted to the legendary Uncle Tom, the old halfwit darky, the white man's jester, the obsequious old white-haired coon without a private thought.

During one of the stops as the long lines of traffic were halted at the toll gates, he hid the shotgun underneath the back seat and tossed the gunman's straw hat on top of the seat.

The toll gates looked like the entrance to a wartime military post housing nuclear weapons. Booted and helmeted cops sat astride high-powered motorcycles beside the toll booths; beyond were the white-and-black police cars that patrolled the tunnel.

The guard took the fifty cents toll and waved Uncle Saint on, but a motorcycle cop strolled over and stopped him.

'What are these holes in the back of this car, boy?'

Uncle Saint grinned, showing stained decayed teeth, and his old bluish-red eyes looked sly.

'Bullet holes, sah,' he said proudly.

'What!' The cop was taken aback; he had expected Uncle Saint to deny it. 'Bullet holes?'

'Yas sah, gen-you-wine bullet holes.'

The cop pinned a beetle-brow stare onto Uncle Saint.

'You make 'em?'

'Naw sah, Ah was goin' the other way.'

The toll guard could not repress a smile, but the cop scowled.

'Who made 'em?'

'My boss, sah. Mistah Jeffers. He made 'em.'

'Who was he shooting at?'

'Shooting at me, sah. He always shoots at me when he's had a liddle too much. But he ain't never hit me though – he-hee.'

The toll guard laughed out loud, but the cop didn't like it.

'Pull over there and wait,' he ordered, indicating the parking space for the patrol cars.

Uncle Saint drove over and stopped. The cops in the cars looked at him curiously.

The motorcycle cop went into the glass-enclosed toll booth and studied the list of wanted cars. The Lincoln was not on the list. He fiddled about for fifteen minutes, looking more and more annoyed. Finally he asked the toll guard, 'Think I ought to hold him?'

'Hold him for what?' the guard said. 'What's an old darky like him ever done but steal his boss's whiskey?'

The cop came out of the booth and waved him on.

It was only a quarter past seven when Uncle Saint came out of the tunnel into Jersey City.

He left the parkway at the first turn-off and went north along the rutted, brick-paved streets that bordered the wharves. He drove slowly and carefully and obeyed all the traffic signs. It took him an hour to reach the first New Jersey approach to the George Washington Bridge. He crossed over into Manhattan and fifteen minutes later crossed the Harlem River back into the Bronx.

Before arriving at Sister Heavenly's he threw out the dead gunman's hat, then retrieved the shotgun, reloaded it, and placed it on the floor of the front seat within reach.

'Now let's see which way the cat's gonna jump,' he said to himself.

It was about 8:30 o'clock. The clock in the car didn't work and Uncle Saint didn't have a watch. But time meant nothing to him one way or another.

7

Grave Digger was sound asleep.

His wife shook him.

'Telephone. It's Captain Brice.'

Grave Digger knuckled the sleep from his eyes. On duty all of his senses were constantly on the alert. Coffin Ed had once summed it up by saying, 'Blink once and you're dead.' To which Grave Digger had rejoined, 'Blink twice and you're buried.'

But at home, Grave Digger relaxed completely. His wife sometimes called him 'Slowpoke.'

He was still sleep-groggy when he took the phone and said grumpily, 'Now what gives?'

Captain Brice was a disciplinarian. He never fraternized with the men under him and played no favorites. The Harlem precinct was his command. Grave Digger and Coffin Ed were under his supervision, although their hours at night rarely permitted them to see him.

'Jake Kubansky is dead,' he said in a voice without inflection. 'I have orders to present you to the commissioner's office at nine o'clock.'

Grave Digger became abruptly alert. 'Has Ed been notified?'

'Yes. I wish we'd had time for you to drop by here and go over this business, but the order just came in. So you had better go straight down to Centre Street.'

Grave Digger looked at his watch. It read 8:10.

'Right, sir,' he said and hung up.

His wife looked at him anxiously. 'Are you in trouble?'

'Not as far as I know.'

That didn't answer her question, but she had learned not to press him.

Grave Digger and Coffin Ed lived only two blocks apart in Astoria, Long Island. Coffin Ed was waiting in his new Plymouth sedan. 'It's going to be another scorcher,' he greeted.

'Let it burn up,' Grave Digger said.

Everyone was in shirtsleeves.

The commissioner, deputy commissioner, inspector in charge of detectives, an assistant D.A., an assistant medical examiner, Captain Brice and Lieutenant Anderson from the Harlem precinct, three firemen and two patrol car cops from the horde who had answered the false fire alarm the previous night.

The hearing was being held in a big barren room in the headquarters annex across the street from the headquarters building. It had begun at 9:55; now it was 11:13. Hard yellow sunlight slanted in from the three windows looking out on Centre Street and the room was sweltering hot.

The charge of 'unwarranted brutality' resulting from the death of Jake had been lodged against Coffin Ed and Grave Digger.

First the assistant M.E. had testified that the autopsy had shown that Jake had died from a ruptured spleen caused by severe external blows in the region of the stomach. In the opinion of the Examiner's Office he had either been kicked in the stomach or pummeled by a heavy blunt instrument.

'I didn't hit him that hard,' Grave Digger had contradicted from where he sat with one ham perched on the window ledge.

Coffin Ed, backed against the wall on the shady side of the room, said nothing.

The commissioner had raised a hand for silence.

Lieutenant Anderson gave a verbal account of the detectives' report and produced photostats of the pages of the precinct blotter where the entry had been made.

Captain Brice explained the special detail to which he had assigned the two detectives, sending them to all trouble spots over Harlem during all hours of the night.

The three firemen and the two patrol car cops testified reluctantly that they had witnessed Grave Digger hit the victim in the stomach while Coffin Ed held his arms pinned behind him.

Then Grave Digger and Coffin Ed had taken the stand in their own defense.

'What we did is routine procedure,' Grave Digger said. 'You take these pushers, when they're peddling dope they work in the street. They carry their decks in a pocket where they are convenient to dispose of. The officer has to apprehend them while they still have the junk on their person, or he has to swear he has seen them dispose of it. So when you close in on a pusher and he sees he can't get rid of his load, he stuffs it into his mouth and eats it. They all carry some kind of physic which they take a short time afterwards – and there goes your evidence –'

The commissioner smiled.

'You know they've been selling dope; you've seen 'em; but you can't prove it,' Grave Digger continued. 'So Ed and me use this method to make them vomit up the evidence before they take the physic and dissipate it.'

Again the commissioner smiled at the use of the word *dissipate*.

'However, if that were permitted, what is there to prohibit an officer from punching a person in the stomach suspected of drunken driving?' the assistant D.A. remarked.

'Nothing,' Grave Digger replied in a thick, dry voice. 'If he's run over somebody and killed 'em.'

'You're forgetting that you are primarily a peace officer,' the asistant D.A. reminded him. 'Your duty is to maintain the peace and the courts will punish the offenders.'

'Peace at what price?' Coffin Ed put in, and Grave Digger echoed thickly:

'You think you can have a peaceful city letting criminals run loose?'

The assistant D.A. reddened. 'That's not the point,' he said sharply. 'You've killed a man suspected of a minor crime, and not in self-defense.'

Suddenly the room was filled with tension.

'You call dope peddling a minor crime?' Grave Digger said, pushing to his feet.

At the sound of his thick, dry voice, every eye in the room turned in his direction. The arteries in his neck became swollen from rage and veins throbbed in his temples.

'All the crimes committed by addicts – robberies, murders, rapes . . . All the fucked-up lives . . . All the nice kids sent down the drain on a habit . . . Twenty-one days on heroin and you're hooked for life . . . Jesus Christ, mister, that one lousy drug has murdered more people than Hitler. And you call it *minor!*' His voice sounded like it was filtered through absorbent cotton.

The assistant D.A. reddened. 'He was merely a peddler,' he stated.

'And who gets it into the victim's blood?' Grave Digger raved. 'The peddler! He sells the dirty crap. He makes the personal contact. He puts them on the habit. He's the mother-raper who gets them hooked. He looks into their faces and puts the poison in their hands. He watches them go down from sugar to shit, sees them waste away. He puts them out to stealing, killing, starts young girls to hustling – to get the money to buy the kicks. I'll take a simple violent murderer any day.'

'Let's put it this way,' Coffin Ed said, trying to mollify both parties. 'Everybody here knows how the big-time operators work. They buy junk abroad – mostly heroin nowadays. They get a lot of it from France – Marseille – for about five thousand dollars a kilo – two pounds and three ounces. The French don't seem to be able to stop the traffic. It comes to New York and the wholesalers pay from fifteen thousand dollars to twenty thousand dollars a kilo for it. The U.S. federal agents don't seem to be able to catch them either. So the wholesalers dilute the stuff, which is about eighty percent pure to begin with – they add enough sugar of milk or quinine to get it down to two percent pure. Just plain shit. And this is the stuff the peddler sells. It grosses a half million dollars a kilo. All of you know that. But who's stopping it? All Digger and me can do is try to catch the peddlers in our precinct. So one gets hurt –'

'Killed,' the assistant M.E. corrected.

'By accident,' Coffin Ed amended. 'If that is what killed him. In all that excitement up there last night he might have been trampled to death for all we know.'

The commissioner looked up. 'What excitement?'

'The firemen were trying to detain a firebug who got away.'

'Oh, that.' His glance flicked from Lieutenant Anderson to the red-faced firemen.

'We are going to have these detectives indicted,' the assistant D. A. stated. 'There has been too much police brutality in Harlem. The public is indignant.'

The commissioner pressed the tips of his fingers together and leaned back in his chair.

'Give us time to make a more thorough investigation,' he said.

The assistant D.A. was reluctant. 'What more investigation is needed? They have admitted beating the deceased.'

The commissioner passed over him. 'In the meantime, detectives Jones and Johnson, you are suspended from the force until further notice. Captain Brice,' he added, turning his head slightly, 'have them turn in their shields and strike their names from the roll.'

Grave Digger's swollen face turned gray around the mouth and the grafted skin on Coffin Ed's face twitched like a tic.

'And that's that,' Grave Digger said to their friend, Lieutenant Anderson, as they stood outside in the glaring hot sunshine. 'For a mother-raping pusher.'

'It's just the newspaper pressure. We're suffering from the customary summer slack in news. It'll blow over,' Lieutenant Anderson consoled. 'The papers are on one of their periodic humanitarian kicks. Don't worry. Nothing's coming out of it.'

'Yeah, humanitarian,' Grave Digger said bitterly. 'It's all right to kill a few colored people for trying to get their children an education, but don't hurt a mother-raping white punk for selling dope.'

Lieutenant Anderson winced. As accustomed as he was to these two colored detectives' racial connotations, that one hurt.

8

Uncle Saint hung about the garage for a long time before he got up enough nerve to enter the house.

Three of the bullets had made holes which he plugged with putty and sprayed with quick-drying black enamel. But there were two big dents and one long seam atop the left rear fender which couldn't be concealed. He had no mirror to replace the broken one, so he removed them from both front fenders and sprayed the marks they had left. That didn't help much either; the bolt holes still remained. The license plates presented no problem. He had several changes of plates, none of which had the legitimate registration number. He put on some Connecticut plates.

Still he kept fiddling about. Once he thought of painting the whole car another color; or at least the upper half. But finally his jag began thinning out and he got jumpy. He knew he'd have trouble sure as hell with Sister Heavenly if he got too jumpy, so he decided to go inside and have it out.

She would just have to look after him, he told himself. She had kept him helpless and homeless for twenty-five years and he wasn't going to jump up and run off by his lonesome just because he was in a little trouble. If he went down he was going to take her with him. It had been her idea anyway, he justified himself. He had just been trying to do her business.

He slunk up the path toward the house, holding the shotgun cradled in his arm as though stalking an enemy.

Only the screen door was closed. He became wary. When he poked his head into the kitchen, his eyes popped. Sister Heavenly was sitting at the kitchen table drinking sassafras tea and smoking a pipe of marijuana and looking content with the world. For a brief moment he thought she had gotten it and his head exploded with rage. But the next instant he realized she couldn't have. He stepped inside and closed the door.

The kitchen had windows on the side and back but their shutters were closed tight to keep out the heat and the only light came in through the screened back door. The kitchen table, covered with blue-and-white checked oilcloth, sat before the side window. The stove stood against the inside wall and Uncle Saint's bunk, covered with army blankets, lay beneath the back window.

Sister Heavenly was dressed as before. She sat sidewise to the table, one leg crossed over the other exposing the ruffles of her petticoats, and her little finger was extended properly as she held the steaming teacup to her lips. Her black beaded bag lay atop the table and her black-and-white striped parasol was propped against the wall beside her.

A small electric fan atop the refrigerator stirred the reeking scent of marijuana and the fragrant aroma of sassafras tea.

She regarded Uncle Saint curiously over the rim of the cup.

'Well, you're finally back,' she said.

Uncle Saint coughed. 'You see me,' he grunted.

Pinky sat across the table from Sister Heavenly, his torso looming so high above her he looked like a barrel-chested midget standing in the chair. He looked from one to the other.

'Did you see Gus?' he asked Uncle Saint in his whining voice.

'I said I would tell you in a minute,' Sister Heavenly snapped at him.

Uncle Saint couldn't make out her game, so he decided to keep his mouth shut. He sat on his bunk, placed the loaded shotgun close beside him, and reached underneath and dragged out a rusty iron lockbox in which he kept everything he owned. From his side pants pocket he took a single key attached to a long brass chain hanging from his belt and unlocked the tremendous Yale padlock which secured his box.

Two pairs of eyes followed his every movement, but he studiedly ignored them. He had his own alcohol lamp, teaspoon and spike, and he would use no other.

Silently they watched him mix a deck of heroin and a deck of cocaine, light the lamp and cook it in a spoon, load the spike. He banged himself in a vein just above his left wrist. His brown decayed teeth bared like an animal's when the spike went in, but his mouth went loose and sloppy in a soft sighing sound as he drew out the spike.

Sister Heavenly finished her cup of tea and waited a few minutes for his speedball to work, slowly swallowing the sweet marijuana smoke.

'What happened to the trunk?' she asked finally.

Uncle Saint looked around as though expecting to find it in the kitchen. He hadn't made up any kind of a story and all his furtive looks at her didn't tell him anything. Outwardly she looked indifferent and serene, but he knew from past experience that didn't mean a thing. Finally he decided to lie to the bitter end. He had lost the mother-raping trunk and had blown some mother-raper's brains out to boot, and wasn't nothing going to change that. He was too mother-raping old to worry about every little thing that came along.

He licked his dry lips and muttered, 'We been barking up the wrong tree. There wasn't nothing in that trunk. Them expressmen come and got it and took it straight to the docks and left it there. I followed them, but when I seen there wasn't nothing in it I figured there had been a switch, so I turned around and highballed it back uptown looking for you, but you has gone. So I figures you has already got it – if there was anything to get.'

'That's what I thought,' she said enigmatically. 'We been on a wild-goose chase.'

Pinky's battered face contorted in a fit of rage. 'You was after Gus's treasure map,' he accused. 'That's why you give me that knockout shot. You was trying to steal Gus's treasure map and you done let him get kilt.'

'He ain't no more dead than you is,' Sister Heavenly said calmly. 'I saw him talking to the expressmen when –'

'You saw Gus alive!' Pinky exclaimed. His eyes bugged out in an expression of horror.

Sister Heavenly went on as though she hadn't noticed. 'Not only saw him but I felt him. He talked to the expressmen when they came for the trunk and gave them the treasure map to mail.'

Pinky stared at her in disbelief. 'You saw Gus give the expressmen the treasure map?' he echoed stupidly.

'What are you so het up about?' she asked sharply. 'Ain't you the one who said he was going to give them the treasure map to mail to him in Ghana?'

'But I thought he was already kilt by now,' Pinky stammered in confusion.

Uncle Saint was staring from one to another with a fixed expression of imbecility. He wondered if he was hearing right.

'He might be killed by now but he was alive when I was there,' she said. 'And Ginny and the African was getting the bags ready to leave. Ginny was straightening up for the new couple what comes in today.'

Pinky looked flabbergasted. He opened his mouth to say

something but was stopped by the sound of an automobile horn from the street in front.

'That's Angelo,' she said casually, and looked sharply from one to the other to see their reactions.

Both looked suddenly guilty and trapped.

She smiled cynically. 'Sit still,' she said. 'I'll go out and see what he wants this early in the morning.'

'But it ain't his day,' Pinky whined.

Uncle Saint threw him a black look.

But Sister Heavenly merely said, 'It sure ain't,' as she got to her feet.

The front door was never opened, so she went out the back door and circled the house by the path. Her long skirt caught in the high dry weeds and burs clung to the hem but she paid it no attention.

A thickset, swarthy, black-haired man wearing a navy blue straw hat with a fluted gray silk band, Polaroid sunglasses in a heavy black frame, a charcoal-gray suit of shantung silk, white silk shirt and knitted maroon tie, sat behind the wheel of a shiny black MGA sports car with white-wall tires. He was a precinct detective sergeant.

Rows of even white teeth showed in his heavily tanned face at sight of her.

'How's tricks, Sister H?' he greeted in a jovial voice.

She rested her black-gloved hands on the door of the car and looked at him questioningly. 'Same as usual.' In the bright sunshine, her black straw hat atop the gray wig glittered like a cockroach.

'Are you sure?' His voice was insinuating.

'Now what do you mean by that?'

'I just came from the station,' he said. 'As soon as I got the reader I came straight to see you. It's the least I could do for an old friend.'

She looked at the dark green lenses of his sunglasses, trying to see his eyes, but she only saw her own reflection. She felt trouble coming on and looked across the street to see if they were being watched.

The villa opposite was the only other house in the block. It was occupied by a large Italian family, but they were so accustomed to seeing the sergeant's flashy car parked in front of Sister Heavenly's, and to all the other strange goings-on in that house, they paid it no attention. At the moment none of the brood was in sight.

'Let's finish with the bullshit,' Sister Heavenly said.

'Finished,' he agreed. 'There was a shotgun killing took place down near the French Line dock at about half past six this morning,' he went on, watching her expression sharply from behind his trick glasses, but her expression didn't change.

'It seems that a man standing on the sidewalk was shotgunned to death by a man sitting in a parked car. They found a derringer with a silencer attached on the sidewalk near the victim. It had recently been fired. Homicide figures the man with the derringer tried to gun the man in the car and got himself shotgunned instead. This sort of rod is a professional's tool. Anyway, the killer got away,' he added offhandedly, waiting for her reaction.

She didn't show any reaction. All she said was, 'What's that mean to me?'

He shrugged. 'Nobody can get any sense out of it. You see, there're a lot of conflicting descriptions of both the car and the killer. All they could get for certain about the car is that it was a black low-slung limousine, but no one knew the make. But there was one guy who described the killer as a little dried-up darky with gray kinky hair who was wearing a chauffeur's uniform; and he can't be shaken.'

'Well, now ain't that lovely!' Sister Heavenly exclaimed in disgust.

'You ain't just saying it,' Angelo agreed. 'Don't make any sense at all. But one thing is for sure. The car is marked. It seems the victim had a friend in a car parked behind the killer's. When this friend saw his buddy shot down he opened up with an automatic and put some holes in the back of the killer's car. That's the lead homicide is following.'

She chewed over that for a time. 'How about this second gunman?' she asked. 'Did he get away too?'

'Nope. That's where the killer got lucky. While this second party was following the killer's car he drove in front of a truck and was run over and killed too.'

A veil dropped over Sister Heavenly's old blue-rimmed ocher eyes as her mind worked furiously. 'Did anybody make them?' she asked.

'Not yet,' he said. 'But they had all the marks of professionals, and they ain't going to be hard to identify.'

'All right,' she conceded finally. 'I got the message. What's it worth?'

He took a small black cheroot from a black leather case which he carried in his breast pocket and slowly applied a flame from a solid gold Flaminaire lighter imported from France. It looked as though he were doing a takeoff on a private eye.

Finally he said, 'Well, Sister H, seeing as how your nephew Pinky is wanted too for putting in that false fire alarm last night, I figure for the two of them together, fifteen C's ain't too much. And while you're at it, you better give me next month's sugar at the same time. With all this shooting going on, who knows where we'll be by then.'

'Two G's!' she exploded. 'Hell, you can have 'em both right now. They ain't worth that much to me.'

He blew out a cloud of smoke and grinned at her. 'You didn't get the message. Homicide is going to wonder what it's all about. They ain't going to bite on the idea that one old darky chauffeur dreamed it up – and nobody else, if you get what I mean.'

She didn't argue. There was no use.

'Let's see if I've got that much,' she said and turned back toward the house.

'Look good and look fast,' he called after her.

She halted and her body stiffened.

'You know this is a lamster's hangout up here in these sticks,' he said. 'And I'm the authority on it. People are going to be asking me questions pretty damn soon, and I got to know how to answer.'

She resumed walking, her long skirts catching in the weeds again as she went around the side of the house. The tethered nanny goat was bleating for water and she stopped for a moment to untie it. Then she kept on through the blistered garden, trampling over the withered vegetables indiscriminately, and looked into the garage. One glance at the Lincoln was enough.

'Who did he think he was fooling,' she murmured to herself, then added half aloud, 'Anyway, I was damn right.'

She returned to the house and entered her bedroom.

Uncle Saint and Pinky had disappeared.

She knelt before the chest of drawers, took out her bunch of keys and selected one and unlocked the bottom drawer. The front of the drawer swung down on hinges, revealing a built-in safe. She spun the dial and opened a small, rectangular door. Then she selected another key and opened an inner compartment which was stuffed with packets of banknotes. She took two packets from the top, closed and locked all three doors and left the room.

A tall, emaciated colored man flashily dressed in a Palm Beach suit and a hard straw hat with a red band stood beside the door. She quickly slipped the money inside of her dress.

'I ain't got no Heavenly Dust now, Slim,' she said. 'Come back later.'

'I need it,' he insisted.

'Well, I ain't got it,' she snapped impatiently, brushing past him toward the sidewalk.

He followed reluctantly. 'When you gonna have it?'

'At one o'clock,' she said over her shoulder.

He looked at his watch. 'It ain't but nine-thirty now. That's three hours and a half,' he whined, following her into the street.

'Beat it,' she snarled.

He looked from her to the detective sitting in the car. Angelo turned his head slightly and made a motion with his thumb. Slim hastened down the street. Angelo watched him in the rearview mirror until he turned into a path across a vacant lot.

'It's clear now,' he said.

Sister Heavenly took the packets of banknotes from inside her dress and placed them in his hand. He counted them carefully without looking up or taking any precaution at concealment. Each packet contained ten one-hundred-dollar notes. Negligently he slipped them into his inside coat pocket.

'Pretty soon you'll be turning in this heap for a Jaguar,' Sister Heavenly said sarcastically.

'You ain't just kidding,' he replied.

The high-powered motor roared into life. She watched him back the car at high speed into the first cross-street, turn and speed away.

Pinky had the key, she thought. But the question was how to get it out of him.

Instead of returning to the kitchen she went on to the rabbit hutch to see if Pinky had taken another speedball in her absence.

The buck rabbit was huddled in a corner of his cage, watching her with terrified eyes. She dragged him out by the ears and removed the stopper from his rectum. The three capsules of C & H that should have been there were gone.

No wonder he was talking so strange, she thought. He must be leaping and flying.

She put the buck back into his cage and walked slowly toward the kitchen, carrying the stopper in her hand.

I'll just play it dumb, she decided, and see what those speed-balls tell him to do next.

9

The house didn't have a basement. It had been built by Italian immigrants unused to the cold winters of the Bronx and who didn't have sufficient money for such a luxury.

Sister Heavenly's bedroom and the kitchen composed one half of the house. The other half was composed of a large front parlor that was kept shuttered and closed and a small back bedroom which Sister Heavenly had converted into a bathroom.

The stairway to the attic led up from the kitchen and took up part of the short front hall, which, like the parlor, was never used. The bottom of the stairway which extended into the kitchen was detachable.

When Sister Heavenly returned to the kitchen she spoke apparently to no one: 'You can come out now, he's gone.'

The bottom of the stairs moved slowly out into the kitchen, revealing an access to a dugout beneath the house.

Pinky's head appeared first. His kinky white hair was covered with cobwebs. On his battered face, ranging in colors from violent purple to bilious yellow, was a look of indescribable stupidity. His shoulders were too large for the opening and he had to put one arm through first and perform a series of contortions. He looked like some unknown monster coming out of hibernation.

The next thing that appeared was Uncle Saint's shotgun, which seemed to drag Uncle Saint behind it.

Pinky shoved the staircase back into place and then stood close to Uncle Saint as though for spiritual comfort.

Neither of them met Sister Heavenly's scornful gaze.

She couldn't restrain from taunting: 'You two innocents are acting mighty strange for people with clear consciences.'

'Ain't no need of going looking for trouble,' Uncle Saint said sheepishly.

Sister Heavenly consulted her old-fashioned locket-watch. 'It's quarter to ten. How about all us going down to the dock and seeing Gus and Ginny off?'

If she had exploded a bomb filled with ghosts, she couldn't have gotten stranger reactions.

Uncle Saint had a sudden heart attack. His eyes rolled back in his head and three inches of tongue fell suddenly from the corner of his dirty-looking mouth. He clutched his heart with his left hand and reeled toward his bunk, taking good care to hold on to the shotgun with his right hand.

Simultaneously Pinky had an epileptic fit. He fell to the floor and had convulsions, contortions and convolutions. His muscles jumped and jerked and quivered as he thrashed about on the floor. Foam sprayed from his mouth.

Sister Heavenly backed quickly from the danger zone of flying legs and arms and took up a position behind the stove.

Pinky's eyes were set in a fixed stare; his spine stiffened, his legs jerked spasmodically, his arms flailed the air like runaway windmills.

Sister Heavenly stared at him in admiration. 'If I had known you could throw wingdings like that I could have been using you all along as a sideline to faith healing,' she said.

Seeing that Pinky was stealing the show, Uncle Saint sat up. His eyes were popping and his jaw was working in awe.

'I'd have never thunk it,' he muttered to himself.

Sister Heavenly looked at him. 'How's your heart attack?'

He avoided her gaze. 'It was just a twinge,' he said sheepishly. 'It's already let up.'

He thought it was a good time to get out and let Pinky carry on. 'I'll go start the car,' he said. 'We might have to take him to the doctor.'

'Go ahead,' Sister Heavenly said. 'I'll nurse him.'

Uncle Saint hastened off toward the garage, still carrying his loaded shotgun. He raised the hood and detached the distributor head, then began to work the starter.

Sister Heavenly could hear the starter above the gritting sounds of Pinky's teeth and realized immediately that Uncle Saint had disabled the car.

She waited patiently.

Pinky's convulsions eased and his body turned slowly rigid. Sister Heavenly stepped over and looked into his staring eyes. The pupils were so distended his eyes looked like red-hot metal balls.

Uncle Saint came in and said the car wouldn't start.

'You stay here and look after Pinky, I'll take a taxi to the docks,' Sister Heavenly decided.

'I'll put some ice on his head,' Uncle Saint said and began fiddling about in the refrigerator.

Sister Heavenly didn't answer. She picked up her black beaded bag and black-and-white striped parasol and went out of the back door.

She didn't have a telephone. She paid for police protection and protected herself from other hazards and her business was strictly cash and carry. So she had to walk to the nearest taxi stand.

Outside she opened the parasol, went around the house by the path through the weeds, and set out walking down the middle of the hot dusty road.

Crouching like an ancient Iroquois, still carrying the loaded shotgun in his right hand, Uncle Saint skulked from corner to corner of the house, watching her. She kept straight on down the street in the direction of White Plains Road without looking back.

Satisfied that she was not coming back, he returned to the kitchen and said to the rigid epileptic on the floor, 'She's gone.'

Pinky jumped to his feet. 'I got to get out of here,' he whined.

'Go ahead. What's stopping you?'

'Looking like I am. The first cop sees me gonna stop me, and I is wanted anyway.'

'Git your clothes off,' Uncle Saint said. 'I'll fix that.'

He seemed possessed with an urgency to be alone.

Sister Heavenly kept to the road until she knew she couldn't be seen from the house, then she turned over to the next street and doubled back.

The house nearest to hers on the same side of the street was in the next block. It was owned by an old Italian couple who lived alone. They were good friends of Sister Heavenly. The man ran a provision house and was away from home during the day.

When Sister Heavenly called, his wife was in the kitchen, straining and bottling wine.

Sister Heavenly asked permission to sit in the attic. She often did this. There was a side window in the attic which offered a clear view of her own house, and whenever she found it necessary to check up on Uncle Saint she sat there watching for an hour or two. The old couple had even provided her with a rocking-chair.

Sister Heavenly climbed the stairs to the attic and, after opening the shutters, settled into her chair.

It was hot enough in the attic to roast a goose, but that didn't bother Sister Heavenly. She liked heat and she never perspired.

She sat rocking gently back and forth, watching the front and back of her own house at the end of the adjoining block.

An hour later Uncle Saint said to Pinky, 'You is dry enough, put on some clothes and git.'

Pinky didn't have a change of clothes in the house and he was more than twice the size of Uncle Saint. The black pants and T-shirt he had taken off were bloodstained and filthy.

'Where am I gonna git some clothes?' he asked.

'Look in the souvenir trunk,' Uncle Saint said.

The souvenir trunk sat beneath a small dormer window in the attic.

'Take a chisel, it's locked,' Uncle Saint added as Pinky started ascending the stairs.

There wasn't any chisel in the kitchen and Uncle Saint wouldn't go to the garage to get one. Pinky couldn't go because he was buck naked, so he took the poker for the stove.

It was an old-fashioned steamer trunk with a domed lid and was bound with wooden hoops. Sunshine slanted on the dust-covered top and when Pinky began prying at the old rusty lock, dust motes filled the air like glittering confetti. All of the windows had been closed after the night's performance to keep out the heat and now the sweaty odor of the dancers lingered in the blazing heat. Pinky began to sweat. Sweat drops splattered in the dust like drops of ink.

'Hey, this stuff is coming off,' he called down to Uncle Saint in a panic.

'That's just the excess,' Uncle Saint reassured him. 'The main part ain't coming off.'

With sudden haste, Pinky levered the poker and the lock flew apart. He raised the lid and looked into the trunk.

The souvenir trunk was where Sister Heavenly kept various garments left by her former lovers when they had lammed. Pinky rummaged about, holding up pants and shirts and cotton drawers with back flaps. Everything was too small. Evidently Sister Heavenly hadn't counted any giants amongst her lovers. But finally Pinky came across a pair of peg-top Palm Beach pants which must have belonged to a very tall man at least. He squeezed into a pair of knee-length cotton drawers and pulled the peg-top trousers over them. They fitted like women's jodhpurs. He looked about until he found a red jersey silk shirt worn by some sharp cat in the early 1930s. It stretched enough for him to get it on. None of the shoes were possible, so he closed the trunk and went down to the kitchen and put on his same old blue canvas sneakers.

'Why didn't yer git a hat?' Uncle Saint said.

Pinky turned around and went back up the stairs and rummaged in the trunk for a hat. The only hat which fitted was a white straw hat with a wide floppy brim and a peaked crown like the hats worn by Mexican peons. It had a black chin strap to keep it on.

'Look around asee if there's some sunglasses,' Uncle Saint called.

There was a shoe box of nothing but sunglasses but the only pair that fitted Pinky had white celluloid frames and plain blue glass lenses. He put them on.

Uncle Saint surveyed his handiwork when Pinky stood before him.

'Not even your own mother would recognize you,' he said proudly, but he called a warning as Pinky started off. 'Keep out the sun or that stuff'll turn purple.'

Sister Heavenly's eyes popped. She stopped rocking and leaned forward.

From out of her own front yard came the blackest man she

had ever seen, and Sister Heavenly had specialized in black men. This man was so black he had blue-and-purple tints to his skin like wet bituminous coal glinting in the sunshine. Not only was he the blackest, but he was the sportiest man she had ever seen. She hadn't seen anyone dressed that sporty since minstrel shows went out.

He was walking fast and there was something about him, especially down around the legs, which reminded her of one of her short-time lovers called Blackberry Slim, but his legs were thicker than Slim's. And that red jersey silk shirt rising from those peg-top legs was identical with one that Dusty Canes used to wear. But that hat – that big white flopping hat with a chin strap, and those blue-tinted sunglasses with a white frame; she had never seen anyone wear a hat like that but Go-Go Gooseman.

'My God!' she exclaimed aloud as she suddenly recognized the man. 'That's Pinky and he's been in my souvenir trunk!'

Her mind started working lightning fast . . . Pinky in disguise. She had expected him to make a move but she hadn't expected to get such a lucky break. Naturally he was headed for the cache.

She jumped up so quickly she overturned the rocking-chair. The old Italian woman tried to stop her in the kitchen to share a bottle of wine but she hurried past and went around the house. She stood behind a green lattice gate and watched Pinky loping past. He didn't look in her direction.

She folded up her parasol to make herself as inconspicuous as possible, and kept well in back of him.

He went directly to the subway stop on White Plains Road and climbed the stairs to the waiting platform. Sister Heavenly was blowing and puffing by the time she reached the turnstile. She acted as though she hadn't recognized Pinky and went down to the other end of the platform.

Looking around he saw her and gave a start. There was no place for him to hide. His only chance was to brazen it out. Everyone was staring at him. Once her gaze wandered in his direction. He stared back at her from behind his blue sunglasses. She looked at him for a moment curiously, then turned as though she had not recognized him and watched the train approach.

Two cars separated them. Both of them remained standing so they could peek around the doors when the train stopped and see if the other was getting off. But neither saw the other peeping.

They rode like this down to Times Square. Pinky jumped off just as the doors were closing. Before Sister Heavenly saw him, the doors were closed. She saw him stop and turn and look directly at her as her coach passed.

She got off at 34th Street and taxied back to Times Square, but he had disappeared. Suddenly she realized that he was trying to outsmart her. He had ridden down to Times Square and had given her the slip on the chance that she might have recognized him. He figured he was throwing her off his tracks. But there was only one place he could have anything cached, and that was the apartment on Riverside Drive.

She hailed a taxi and told the driver to step on it.

The driver leaned over a little to peer at her through the rear-view mirror. My God, she's still trying, he thought. But all the time she's already had, if she ain't made it yet she'll never make it now.

Sister Heavenly had him stop in front of Riverside Church. She got out and paid him. He paused for a moment to watch her, making as though he was writing in his record sheet. He was curious. She had rushed him up here as though it were a matter of life and death, and all she wanted was to go to church.

Some of these old ladies think all God has got to do is wait on them, he thought sourly and shifted into gear.

Sister Heavenly waited until he had driven out of sight. Then she walked across the street into the park and selected a bench where she could watch the entrance to the apartment unobserved unless Pinky deliberately looked about for her.

Whistles began to blow as she took her seat. She pulled out her locket-watch to see if it was correct. It read twelve noon on the dot.

It was twelve noon sharp when Coffin Ed turned his Plymouth sedan into the northbound stream of traffic on lower Broadway.

'What do two cops do who've been kicked off the force?' he asked.

'Try to get back on,' Grave Digger said in his thick, cotton-dry voice.

He didn't say another word all the way uptown; he sat burning in a dry, speechless rage.

It was twelve-thirty when they checked into the Harlem precinct station to turn in their shields to Captain Brice.

They stood for a moment on the steps of the precinct station, watching the colored people pass up and down the street, all citizens of Harlem who stepped out of the way to let the white cops by who had business in the station.

The vertical rays of the sun beat down.

'First thing to do is find Pinky,' Grave Digger said. 'All we had on Jake is possession. If we get evidence he was peddling H too, that might give us a start.'

'He's got to talk,' Coffin Ed pointed out.

'Talk! TALK! You think he ain't going to talk! Much as you and me need a few kind words. Ain't no mother-raper who ever knew Jake going to refuse to do a little talking.'

Fifteen minues later they pulled up before the apartment on Riverside Drive.

'Do you see what I see?' Coffin Ed remarked as they alighted.

'There couldn't be but one of 'em,' Grave Digger said.

The dog was lying in front of the iron gate to the rear entrance. It lay on its side with its back to the gate and all four feet extended. It seemed to be asleep. The vertical rays of the midday sun beat down on its tawny hide.

'It must be cooking in this heat,' Coffin Ed said.

'Maybe she's dead.'

It still wore the heavy muzzle reinforced with iron and the brass-studded collar with the chain attached.

They walked toward it by common accord.

Its lambent eyes half opened as they approached and a low growl, like distant thunder, issued from its throat. But it didn't move.

Green flies were feeding from a dirty open wound in its head from which black blood oozed.

'The African did a poor job,' Grave Digger observed.

'Maybe he was in a hurry to get back.'

Grave Digger reached down and took hold of the chain close to the collar. The rest was underneath the dog. He pulled gently and the dog climbed slowly to her feet in sections, like a camel getting up. She stood groggily, looking disinterested.

'She's about done in,' Coffin Ed said.

'You'd be done in too if you were knocked in the head and thrown in the river.'

The dog followed docilely as they went back to the front entrance and rang the superintendent's bell. There was no answer. Coffin Ed stepped over to the mailboxes and pushed buttons indiscriminately.

The latch clicked with a ratchetlike sound that went on and on.

'Everyone's expecting.'

'Looks like it.'

As they were descending the stairs to the basement, Coffin Ed said curiously, 'What do we do if we run into trouble?'

They were still in their shirtsleeves and they had left their revolvers at home that morning.

'Pray,' Grave Digger said thickly, the rage building up in him again. 'Don't forget we're subject to the charge of impersonating officers if we claim to be cops.'

'How can I forget it,' Coffin Ed said bitterly.

The first thing they noticed was that the trunk was gone.

'Looks like we're too late.'

Grave Digger said nothing.

There was no reply to the janitor's bell. Grave Digger looked at the Yale lock above the old-fashioned mortise lock. He passed the dog's chain to Coffin Ed to hold and took a Boy Scout's knife from his pants pocket.

'Let's just hope the night lock ain't on,' he said, opening the screwdriver blade.

'Let's just hope we don't get caught, you mean,' Coffin Ed amended, turning to watch all the entrances.

Grave Digger forced the blade between the doorjamb and the lock, slowly forced back the bolt and pushed open the door.

Both of them grunted from shock.

The body of the African was lying in a grotesque position in the center of the bare linoleum floor with its throat cut from ear to ear The wound had stopped bleeding and the surrounding blood had coagulated, giving the impression of a purple-lipped monster's mouth.

Blood was everywhere, over the furniture, the floor, the African's white turban and crumpled robe.

For a moment there was only the sound of their labored breathing and the buzzing of an electric fan somewhere out of sight.

Then Coffin Ed reached behind him, knocking the dog aside, and closed the door. The sound of the clicking of the lock released them from their trance of shock.

'Whoever did that wasn't joking,' Grave Digger said soberly, the anger drained from him.

'As many as I've seen, I always get a shock,' Coffin Ed confessed.

'Me too. This mother-raping senseless violence!'

'Yeah, but what you gonna do?' Coffin Ed said, thinking about themselves.

'Hell, meet it is all.'

The dog inched forward unnoticed and suddenly Coffin Ed looked down and saw it sniff at the cut throat and lick the blood.

'Get back, Goddammit!' he shouted, snatching up the chain.

The dog backed up and cringed.

Finally they got around to noticing that the room was in a shambles. Rugs were scattered; drawers were emptied, the contents strewn about the floor; the stuffed birds and animals had been gutted, the statuettes smashed, the overstuffed furniture slashed and the packing ripped apart; the broken-down TV sets and the radio had been pried open, the housing of the organ bashed in.

Without commenting, Coffin Ed looped the handle of the dog chain over the doorknob. Then he and Grave Digger poked into the other rooms, taking care not to step into the blood. Doors led from the parlor into the kitchen and one bedroom, beyond which was a bathroom. There was the same disorder in all. They went back and stared at the body of the African.

The macabre hideousness of the bloody corpse was accentuated by the buzzing of the fan. Grave Digger bent over and sent his gaze along the floor, underneath the bloodstained shattered furniture, searching for it. The fan lay overturned beneath the dining table, half hidden by a broken television screen. He located the wall socket and jerked out the plug.

Silence came down. It was the dinner hour and the basement was deserted.

They could almost hear their thoughts moving around.

'If what the janitor's wife said about Pinky is true, he might have cut the African's throat.' Coffin Ed spoke his thoughts aloud.

'I don't figure him for this,' Grave Digger said. 'What would he be looking for?'

'Search me. What about her? Cat-eyed women are known for cutting throats.'

'And search her own house?' Grave Digger said.

'Who knows? All this heat is affecting people's minds. Maybe she thought her husband had something hidden here.'

'Why would she kill the African? It looked to me like they were cooking with the same gas. It was obvious he was laying her.'

'I don't dig this at all,' Coffin Ed confessed. 'Somebody wanted something bad, but they didn't find it.'

'That's obvious. If they had found it, there would be at least one small place that wasn't torn up, some indication where the search had stopped.'

'But what the hell could they be looking for important enough to murder? What could one old colored janitor have that valuable?'

Grave Digger began considering the sex angle. 'You think he's that old? Old enough to kill the African out of jealousy? Or you think he found out they were crossing him in some way?'

'I ain't figuring him for doing it. But it figures he was old. And old men don't generally take chances.'

'Who told you that?'

'Anyway, there're a hell of a lot of questions here need answering,' Coffin Ed said.

With unspoken accord, they approached the body, picking their way through the blood. Coffin Ed grimaced and his face began to twitch.

Grave Digger lifted one of the African's arms, holding the wrist between his thumb and first finger, then let it drop. The body was still limp even though the blood had coagulated.

'How do you account for that?' Coffin Ed asked.

'Maybe it's the heat. In weather this hot it might take some time for rigor mortis to set in.'

'It might be that he ain't been dead long too.'

They looked at one another with the same sudden thought. A chill seemed to come into the room.

'You think he came in and interrupted the search? And that's why he got killed?'

'It figures,' Coffin Ed said.

'Then the chances are the murderer might not have finished when we arrived.'

'Or *they*. It don't have to be just one person.'

'In that case they might still be hiding somewhere in this basement.'

Coffin Ed didn't reply immediately. The grafted patches of skin on his face contorted and the tic set in.

For a time they stood without moving, holding their breath to listen. Vague sounds drifted in from the street – passing automobiles, the distant horn of a ship, the muted, unidentifiable thousand sounds of the city forming an unnoticeable undertone. The rat-tat-tat of a woman's heels hurrying down the hallway overhead was followed by the rumbling of the elevator starting. But no sound came from the vicinity of the basement. It was a quiet residential street and during this hour most of the tenants, grownups and children alike, were at lunch.

At the same time both were trying to reconstruct the layout of the basement from what little they had seen of it. On their previous visit they had noticed that the laundry was to the right of the back entrance facing a corridor which ran parallel to the back wall. Next to the laundry were the elevator, staircase to the front hall, a toolroom and the door to the janitor's suite; all of which faced the blank whitewashed wall of the storeroom entered from the other side. Another hall running parallel with the front of the house turned off at right angles at the janitor's door and no doubt continued around the other side of the house, encircling the basement. They had both noticed that the door to the boiler room opened off the front hall.

'I'd feel a hell of a lot better if I was heeled,' Grave Digger confessed.

'I got a notion we're making rattlesnakes out of tadpoles,' Coffin Ed said.

'Let's play it safe,' Grave Digger said. 'Whoever cut this boy's throat wasn't kidding.'

Coffin Ed unhooked the dog's chain from the doorknob, cracked the door and peered cautiously down the corridor.

'This situation is funny,' he said. 'Here we are, supposed to be tough cops, and are scared to poke our heads out of this door in the basement of one of the safest houses in the city.'

'You call this safe?' Grave Digger said, indicating the gory stiff. 'And it wouldn't be so funny if you got your head blown off.'

'Well, we can't stay holed up like two rats,' Coffin Ed said and threw open the door.

Grave Digger leaped to one side and flatted himself against the wall flanking the door, but Coffin Ed stood out in the open.

'You remind me of a Spanish captain I read about in a book

by Hemingway,' Grave Digger said disgustedly. 'This captain figured the enemies were all dead so he charged the dugout single-handed, beating his chest and yelling at them to come out and shoot him, showing how brave he was. And you know what – one of 'em rose up and shot him through the heart.'

'Does that look like any enemy is out there?' Coffin Ed demanded.

In both directions, the brightly lit, whitewashed corridors were deserted and serene. The door to the laundry was open but the doors to the toolroom and boiler room were closed. But they had wire mesh in the place of upper panels and not a sound came from either room. It looked as peaceful as a grave. The idea of killers lurking in ambush seemed suddenly absurd.

'Hell, I'm going to look around,' Coffin Ed said.

But Grave Digger was still for playing it safe. 'Not without a gun, man,' he cautioned again. Suddenly he was struck by an idea. 'Let's send out the dog to sniff around.'

Coffin Ed glanced at her scornfully. 'She couldn't hurt a mouse with that muzzle on.'

'I'll fix that,' Grave Digger said and stepped over to the bitch and removed the muzzle and unhooked the chain.

He pushed her out into the corridor but she merely looked over her shoulder at him as though she wanted to come back in. He looked about for something to throw but everything movable was bloody, so he took off his hat and sailed it down the corridor in the direction of the boiler room door.

'There, boy, there, boy, go get it,' he urged.

But the bitch suddenly turned around with her tail between her legs and ran into the kitchen. They could hear her lapping up water.

'I'm going to call homicide,' Grave Digger said. 'Have you seen a phone?'

'In the kitchen.'

'That's a house phone.'

Coffin Ed stepped outside and looked up and down the corridors. 'Here's a pay phone beside the door. You got a dime?'

Grave Digger fished some change from his pocket. 'Yeah.'

It was an old-fashioned telephone box attached to the wall with the mouthpiece on a level with the average man's mouth. Grave Digger stepped around the corner, lifted the receiver and put in a dime. He held the receiver to his ear, waiting for the dial tone.

'I'm going to get a couple of wrenches or something we can use for saps, just in case,' Coffin Ed said, stepping over toward the toolroom.

'Why don't you let it alone and let's just wait for some cops with pistols,' Grave Digger called over his shoulder.

But Coffin Ed thought better. He pushed open the toolroom door and leaned inside, reaching for the light switch.

He never knew what hit him. Lights exploded in his head as though his brain had been dynamited right behind the eyes.

Grave Digger had just gotten the dial tone and had stuck his right index finger on the figure 7 when he heard the flat whacking sound made by the impact of a blunt instrument against a human skull. There could be no mistaking the sound; he had heard it often enough. He was moving, his head wheeling and ducking, before the sound of the following grunt reached his ears.

He never got around but his head had moved enough so that the bullet intended for his temple struck the guttapercha receiver in his left hand, shattered it but was deflected so that it merely burned a blister across the back of his neck.

The gunman was a marksman with a pistol. He was using a derringer with a sawed-off barrel and a silencer attached, similar to the one used by the gunman whom Uncle Saint had killed. At the sound of Coffin Ed opening the toolroom door, he had stepped from the boiler room into the corridor and had taken a bead on Grave Digger's head, resting the meat side of his trigger hand in the crook of his raised left arm. But even the best of marksmen could miss with a one-shot gun, so he also held a .38-caliber police positive in his left fist as insurance.

Grave Digger's left hand and the whole left side of his head went numb and he felt as though he had been kicked in the head by a mule. But he was not stunned. He erupted into motion like the snapping of a clock spring. He went down into a rolling plunge toward the open door of the janitor's suite.

He wasn't looking toward the gunman; his eyes, his mind, his straining muscles, and all his five senses were concentrating on escape. But somehow his mind retained the impression of a face – a dead-white, death's head face with colorless lips pulled back from small yellow teeth and huge deep-set eyes like targets on a pistol range: black balls rimmed with a thin line of white about which were large irregular patches of black – a hophead's face.

The gunman straightened out his left arm and fired the police positive.

The bullet caught Grave Digger in his spin as he was turning on a long slant, almost horizontal to the floor. It went in underneath the left shoulder blade and came out three inches above the heart.

Grave Digger grunted once like a stuck hog and was knocked flat on his face. But he didn't lose consciousness. He felt his face skidding across the slick cool surface of linoleum and he knew he had got inside the room. With a quick convulsive movement which consumed the last of his strength, he rolled over on his back like a cat turning in midair and kicked with his left foot toward the door, trying to close it. He missed it and his foot was in the air. His stabbing, desperate gaze went across it, and he found himself looking straight down the barrel of the police positive.

He thought fleetingly, without fear or regret, Digger, your number's up.

That's the last he knew.

Hopped to the gills, the gunman stalked forward on the balls of his feet to place another slug in the absolutely motionless body, but the second gunman, standing by the toolroom door, shouted, 'For chrissakes, cummon, Goddammit! Did you have to use that sonofabitching cannon?'

The hopped-up gunman paid him no attention. He was intent on pumping another slug into his victim.

But suddenly a woman let out a scream. It was a scream of unbelievable volume and immeasurable terror. You could tell it was a colored woman screaming by the heart she put into it. It was the loudest screaming the hopped-up gunman had ever heard and it shattered his control like glass breaking.

He started to run blindly and without direction. He ran head-long into the second gunman, who grappled with him and they struggled furiously for a brief moment.

The colored maid was standing as she had stepped from the elevator. The basket of soiled clothes lay overturned on the floor where it had fallen from her hands. Her body was rigid. Her mouth formed an ellipsoid big enough to swallow an ostrich egg, showing the chewing edges of her molars, a white-coated tongue flatted between the bottom teeth and humped in the back against the tip of a palate which hung down like a blood-red stalagmite. Her neck muscles were corded. Her popeyed stare was fixed. Screams kept pouring from her mouth with an unvarying, nerve-shattering resonance.

The second gunman got his left arm free and slapped the hopped-up gunman twice across the face.

Sanity returned to the dilated pupils, along with terror. He holstered the police positive in a right-shoulder sling, dropped the derringer into his right coat pocket, and went up the stairs as though the furies were after him.

'Not so fast, you hophead bastard!' the second gunman called from behind him. '*Walk* out into the street.'

II

The *Queen Mary* sailed at twelve noon sharp.

Wharf attendants said they had never witnessed so much confusion at the sailing of a Cunard Line ship.

Two of the tugboats on hand to ease the big ship from its mooring ran together. An able-bodied seaman was knocked into the drink and one of the tugboat captains choked on his false teeth.

Two stout businessmen celebrating the departure of their wives, along with a fat lady seeing off her daughter, fell off the dock and the *Queen* had to backwater until they were fished out.

The dock police trying to keep the people behind the guard lines were mobbed. Fights broke out; several people were trampled.

Fifteen hundred passengers were on board and five thousand people on the dock to see them off. With the blowing of the tugboat whistles, the shouting of orders, the screaming of good-byes from six thousand five hundred throats, there was enough noise to arouse the inhabitants of a cemetery.

Authorities said it was due to the excessive heat. The threat of a thunderstorm had passed over and the sun beat down from a cloudless sky.

In the general confusion, no one gave Pinky a second glance. An international atmosphere prevailed; thoughts dwelled on faraway places and people. Those who saw him put him down as either an African politician, a Cuban revolutionary, a Brazilian snake charmer, or just a plain ordinary Harlem shoeshine boy.

Pinky was looking for the trunk.

While everyone's attention was directed to the confusion on the dock, he looked through the pile of freight inside the shed at the end of the wharf.

One of the guards came back and caught him there.

'What you doing in here, boy? You know you ain't got any business here.'

'I'm looking for Joe,' Pinky said, ducking and dodging like a halfwit to divert the guard's suspicions.

Like all colored people, Pinky knew if he acted stupid enough the average white man would pass him off as a harmless idiot.

The guard looked at Pinky and suppressed a smile.

Pinky was sweating and where the dye had run he had big purple splotches across the back of his red jersey silk shirt, down the front, underneath the arms and on the seat of his Palm Beach pants. Sweat was running down his face, collecting on the knot of his chin strap to his hat and dripping to the floor.

'Joe who?' the guard asked.

'Joe the porter. You know Joe.'

'Look upstairs where they keep the passenger luggage; porters don't work here,' the guard said.

'Yassah,' Pinky said and shuffled off.

A moment later the guard told a co-worker who had come over to join him, 'See that darky there?' He pointed. 'The one in the white hat and red shirt going upstairs.'

The second guard looked dutifully.

'He's sweating ink,' the first guard said.

The second guard smiled indulgently.

'I mean it,' the first guard said. 'Look there on the floor. That's where he sweated.'

The second guard looked at the purple blots on the gray concrete floor and grinned unbelievingly.

The first guard grew indignant. 'You don't believe it? Go look at him for yourself.'

The second guard conceded with a nod.

The first guard relaxed. 'I've heard of darkies sweating ink,' he said. 'But this is the first time I've ever seen it.'

Pinky saw the trunk the moment he approached the section for the luggage that went aboard ship. All the luggage that had surrounded it had been loaded and it stood by itself.

He didn't go near it. He seemed satisfied just by the sight of it.

The next thing was to find the African.

He took up a station behind a concrete pier underneath the railroad trestle and watched the people as they left the wharf. He didn't anticipate any difficulty in locating him among the throng. He gonna look like a fly in a glass of buttermilk, he thought.

But after an hour he gave it up. If the African had been there to see Gus and Ginny off, he would have left by then.

He decided to go uptown and check with the African's landlady. If he lost the African he was going to be caught holding the bag.

The African had a room at 145th Street and Eighth Avenue. The hell of it was how to get there without getting nabbed by the cops. It had occurred to him that he was beginning to look conspicuous with the dye running all over his clothes. Besides which he didn't have but fifteen cents, and he couldn't take a taxi if he had found a driver willing to take him.

While he was giving this some thought an old sandwichman shuffled along the sidewalk opposite the wharves, looking wistfully into all the bars he passed. Pinky's mind was cool and sharp from the four speedballs he had loaded his veins with that morning.

He read the advertisement on the signboards hanging fore
and aft the old man's shoulders:

BLINSKY'S BURLESQUE
in
Jersey City
50 *Beautiful Girls* 50
10 *Glamorous Striptease Artistes* 10
6 *Zippy Comedians* 6
GREATEST DISPLAY ON EARTH

Underneath some wit had written in red drawing crayon:

Beats Picasso

Pinky studied the old man, took in the battered straw hat, the
bulbous red nose, the white stubble of two days' whiskers, the
ragged cuffs of baggy pants and the beat-up shoes with one sole
flapping loose showing beneath the signboards. He tabbed him
as a bum from Hoboken.

He cut across the traffic lane and approached the old bum.

'Is it true what they say?' he asked, shuffling from one foot to
another and acting like a natural son of Uncle Tom. 'Ah just come
from Mississippi and Ah wants to know is it true.'

The old bum looked up at him from rheumy eyes.

'Is what true, Sam?' he said in a whiskey voice.

Pinky licked his purple lips with his big pink tongue. 'Is it true
all them white women shows theyself mother naked?'

The old bum grinned, exposing a couple of dung-colored
snaggleteeth.

'Mother naked!' he croaked. 'They ain't even that. They done
shaved off the feathers.'

'Ah sho do wish Ah could see 'em,' Pinky said.

That gave the bum an idea. He had been down there all morning hustling up trade among the truck drivers and long-shoremen, and the barmen wouldn't even let him enter the bars wearing his sign.

'You hold this sign while I go inside and see a friend and I'll see what I can do for you,' he promised.

'Ah sho will,' Pinky said, helping the old bum pull the boards up over his head.

The old bum beat it for the nearest bar and disappeared inside. Pinky took off in the opposite direction and turned out of sight at the first corner. Then he stopped and hooked the boards over his head. It was a tight fit and the boards stuck out back and front like some newfangled water wings, but he felt covered. He walked toward Columbus Circle to catch the Broadway subway without any qualms.

He got off at 145th Street and Lenox Avenue. As soon as he came up from the subway kiosk, he took off the sandwich boards. He was in Harlem now and he didn't need them anymore.

He walked to Eighth Avenue and started to enter a doorway to one side of the Silver Moon Bar.

'*Pst, pst,*' someone called from the adjoining doorway.

He looked around and saw an old colored woman beckoning to him. He went over to see what she wanted.

'Don't go in there,' she warned him. 'They's two white 'lice-men in there.'

She didn't know him from Adam's tomcat, but it was the rigid code of colored people in Harlem to stick together against white cops; they were quick to warn one another when white cops were around, there was no telling who might be wanted.

He looked around for the prowl car, tensed and ready to take off.

'They's plainclothes dicks,' she elaborated. 'And they snuck up here in that ordinary-looking Ford.'

He gave one look at the parked Ford sedan and took off down Eighth Avenue without waiting to thank her. His real cool brain was thinking up a breeze. He figured the only reason two white dicks could be in that tenement at that particular time was they were looking for the African. That was just what he wanted. The only thing wrong was they were looking for the African too soon. That meant they had got something on the African he didn't know about.

After covering two blocks he figured it was safe enough to turn into a bar. Then he remembered he didn't have any money, so he had to keep on down to 137th Street where he had a friend who ran a tobacco shop as a front for a numbers drop and a connection where the pushers dropped by and sold teen-age schoolkids sticks of marijuana and doctored-up decks of heroin.

His friend was an old man called Daddy Haddy who had white leprous-looking splotches on his leathery tan skin. It was choking hot in the small, dark, musty shop but Daddy Haddy wore a heavy brown sweater and a black beaver hat pulled down low enough to touch the rims of his black smoked glasses. He looked at Pinky without a sign of recognition.

'What you want, Mac?' he asked suspiciously in a high falsetto voice.

'What's the matter with you?' Pinky said angrily. 'You going blind? Can't you see I is Pinky?'

Daddy Haddy looked at him through his smoked glasses. 'You is ugly as Pinky,' he admitted. 'And you got the size for it. But what is you doing in that skin? You fall in some blackberry juice?'

'I dyed myself. The cops is looking for me.'

'Git out of here, then,' Daddy Haddy said in alarm. 'You want to get me knocked off?'

'Ain't nobody seen me come in here, and you seen for yourself that don't nobody know me,' Pinky argued.

'Well, say what you want and then beat it,' Daddy Haddy conceded grudgingly. 'The way that dye is running you ain't going to be blue for long.'

'All I want you to do is send Wop up to the corner of 145th Street to look out for a African and warn him not to go back home 'cause the police is looking for him.'

'Umph!' Daddy Haddy grunted. 'How he going to know a African from anybody else?'

'This African don't look like nobody else. He wear a white head rag and a Mother Hubbard dress in four different colors over his pants.'

'What's he done?'

'He ain't done nothing. That's how he dress all the time.'

'I mean done for the police to be looking for him.'

'How I know what he's done,' Pinky whined irritably. 'I just don't want him to get caught yet.'

'Besides which, Wop is high,' Daddy Haddy said. 'He's so high everything looks like four colors to him and he's liable to stop some old woman, thinking she's the African.'

'I thought you was my friend,' Pinky whined.

The old man looked at his purple-dyed face knotting up and gave the matter a second thought.

'Wop!' he shouted.

A coal-black boy, wafer thin, with a long egg-shaped head and slanting eyes, came in from the back room. He wore the white T-shirt, blue jeans and canvas sneakers of any other black boy his age in Harlem. The difference was he had long, straight black hair and there were no whites to his obsidian eyes.

'What you want?' he asked in a gruff, unpleasant voice.

'You tell him,' Daddy Haddy said.

Pinky gave him the picture.

'What if the 'licemens already got him?' Wop asked.

'Then you hightail it away from there.'

'All right,' Wop said. 'Press the skin.'

'I'll see you tonight at Sister Heavenly's,' Pinky promised. 'If I ain't there I'll leave a sawbuck with Uncle Saint.'

'All right, daddy-o,' Wop said. 'Don't make me have to look for you.'

He took a pair of smoked glasses from his blue jeans, fitted them to his head, put both hands into his hip pockets and opened the door with his foot and stepped out into the light.

'Don't bet too much on him,' Daddy Haddy warned.

'I ain't,' Pinky said and followed Wop outside.

They went off in opposite directions.

12

'I know she got it,' Uncle Saint muttered to himself as he dug up the half-pint bottle of nitroglycerin he had buried in the garage. 'Trying to look so innocent that butter wouldn't melt in her mouth. Think she can con old Uncle Saint. Long as I has knowed that double-crossing bitch.'

He muttered to himself as he worked. He was in a driving hurry, but he had to be careful with the stuff. Only five minutes had elapsed since Pinky left the house, but there was no telling when Sister Heavenly would return and he had to have it and gone by then.

'Don't believe anymore she's going down to see Gus off than I believe in Santa Claus,' he muttered. 'The truth ain't in that lying bitch. She's just as soon gone down to sell me to the police for some more protection as she is to have gone to fence the stuff, whatever it is.'

The nitroglycerin was in a green glass bottle filled to the tip and closed securely with a rubber stopper to make it airtight. He had buried it there fifteen years before when she had started thinking about getting rid of him because one of her lovers had objected to having him around.

'She going to get rid of me all right,' he muttered. 'But she going to pay for twenty-five years of service.'

He had wrapped the bottle in a section of rubber inner tube, binding it with a roll of adhesive tape. The ground had hardened during fifteen years and the bottle seemed to have gone in deeper. He dug at first with a spade, measuring the excavation with a wooden folding ruler. He had buried it two feet deep. When he got down to twenty inches he discarded the spade and began digging with a kitchen spatula. But he had to go another ten inches before he scraped the top of the package and it had been slow work with the spatula. Time was passing. Sweat poured from him like showers of rain. He still wore the ancient chauffeur's uniform and cap and he felt like he was inside a coke oven.

But now he worked very carefully, scraping the dirt from around the rotten package with a kitchen spoon.

Both the tape and the rubber had disintegrated and came away from the bottle like rotten cork. He went to extreme pains not to touch the bottle with the spoon.

'Wouldn't that bitch be happy?' he muttered. 'Come home and find me gone. Wouldn't even have to bury me. Just have to fan away the dust.'

Finally the green bottle was uncovered. When he lifted it carefully, inch by inch from its resting place, the top of the rubber stopper fell away, but a thin layer remained covering the nitroglycerin. He held his breath until he straightened it right side up, then he gave a deep sigh.

The loaded shotgun lay on the ground beside him. Holding the bottle of nitroglycerin in his right hand, he reached out with his left hand and picked up the shotgun, then got to his feet like a weight-lifter arising with two tons of steel.

He didn't want the nitroglycerin to get in the sunshine so he held it over his heart beneath his coat. Sweat trickled from the band of his chauffeur's cap and stung his eyes as he picked his way across the uneven surface of the dried-up garden like a tightrope walker crossing Niagara Falls.

When he came to the kitchen door, he propped the shotgun against the wall and opened the door with his right hand, making a complete turn to step into the kitchen to be certain of not bumping the edge of the door with the bottle. Inside he eased the door shut and looked about for a place to set the bottle. The kitchen table looked as safe as anywhere. He placed it on the center of the top of the oilcloth cover.

Now he had to go back to the garage for another package containing an electric drill with a ⅜-inch diamond-pointed bit, a 12-inch length of fuse, and two feet of ¼-inch rubber tube.

The package was wrapped in a plastic doily and hidden inside of an old tire hanging from the rafters. He had gotten hold of these things eleven years after he had buried the nitroglycerin, during his second serious crisis with Sister Heavenly. That one had resulted from Sister Heavenly's conclusion that his hanging around was the chief reason she was so unsuccessful in getting a reliable new lover.

He had only left the kitchen for a few minutes, but during his absence the nanny goat had opened the screen door and entered and was in the act of eating the oilcloth table cover. She had eaten a hole several inches deep, pulling the cover toward the edge as she ate. The bottle of nitroglycerin had been moved more than six inches and was perilously nearing the edge, but it still remained upright.

She was just about to take another bite when he cried, 'Hah!' She paused and looked at him through her cold yellow eyes, then turned back to continue eating.

He jerked up the muzzle of the shotgun and aimed it at her head. 'Git away from there or I'll blow your mother-raping head off,' he said in a dry, dangerous voice.

Sweat broke out in the palms of his hands, but he didn't dare shoot.

Slowly the goat turned her head about and looked at him. The goat didn't know he was scared to shoot. He looked to her like he was going to shoot and she believed him.

Maintaining her dignity, she turned and walked daintily from the kitchen, pushing the door open with her head. And he didn't dare kick her in the rear.

He moved the bottle of nitroglycerin back to the center of the table and placed the other package beside it. Then he sat on his bunk and pulled out his lockbox, unlocked the big padlock, took out his lamp and spoon, and cooked a shot of straight heroin to calm his nerves. His hands were trembling violently and his mouth was working but no sound was issuing forth.

'Ahhhh!' he moaned as he banged himself straight into the vein at the wrist.

He put away his paraphernalia, locked the box and pushed it beneath the bunk, and sat waiting for the drug to take effect.

'How she got it? What I care?' he started muttering again to himself. 'That tricky bitch could steal the cross from under Christ without him ever missing it.' He let out a dry cackling laugh. 'But old Uncle Saint going to out-trick her.'

By then his hands had steadied and his head was filled with a sense of omniscience. He felt as though he could make a *four* by two deuces with the first roll of the dice.

He stood up and opened the package, fitted the bit into the electric drill. Holding it in his right hand, he stepped over to the bunk and retrieved his shotgun with his left hand, and went into Sister Heavenly's bedroom.

He placed the shotgun on the floor in front of the chest of drawers, then unplugged the cord to the bed lamp to plug in the cord to his drill.

The outside lock didn't give him any trouble. He bored a series of holes around it until the flap fell forward. Then he began drilling a hole into the safe about an inch to the right of the dial. The hard safe-steel didn't give like butter; it had almost worn the diamond point from the bit before it broke through.

Now came the ticklish part. He inserted the ¼-inch tube into the ⅜-inch hole until it struck bottom inside of the door. More than a foot hung out. He cut it off so that only an inch protruded. Then he made a funnel out of a sheet of white writing paper and fitted the small end into the rubber tube.

He went back to the kitchen and picked up the bottle of nitroglycerin and took it into the bedroom. With the end of a safety pin he fished out the thin layer of rubber in the neck of the bottle. With infinite precaution, holding his breath all the while, he emptied the bottle into the funnel, pouring in a thin steady stream. When it was finished he stood the empty bottle on the floor and let out his breath in a long heartfelt sigh.

Now he began feeling elated. He had it made now. He removed the funnel and fitted the fuse into the end of the rubber tube. He started to gather up the drill and bit and the empty bottle, but then he thought, 'What the hell for?'

He picked up his loaded shotgun and started to strike a match. He heard someone at the kitchen door. He swung the shotgun around and cocked both barrels and stepped into the kitchen. But it was only the nanny goat trying to get back inside. In a sudden squall of rage, he reversed the gun and started to club her across the head. But he was struck by a sudden idea.

'You want to come in, come on in,' he muttered and opened the door wide for her to enter.

She stared at him appraisingly, then came inside slowly and looked around as though she had never been there before.

He chuckled evilly as he returned to the bedroom and struck the match. The goat followed him out of curiosity and was bending her neck to peer around his leg when he lit the fuse. He hadn't seen the goat follow him into the bedroom. The instant the fuse began to burn he wheeled about and started to run. The goat thought he was after her and wheeled about to run also. But she wheeled the wrong way, and he didn't see her until it was too late. He tripped over her and fell face forward toward the floor.

'Goat, beware!' he cried as he was falling.

He had forgotten to uncock the shotgun, which he still held with the butt forward as when he had intended clubbing her in the head.

The butt struck the floor and both barrels went off. The heavy charge of buckshot struck the front of the safe, behind which was one-half pint of nitroglycerin.

Strangely enough, the house disintegrated in only three directions – forward, backward and upward. The front went out across the street, and such items as the bed, tables, chest of drawers and a handpainted enamel chamber pot crashed into the front of the neighbor's house. Sister Heavenly's clothes, some of which dated back to the 1920s, were strewn over the street like a weird coverlet of many colors. The back of the house, along with the kitchen stove, refrigerator, table and chairs, Uncle Saint's bunk and lockbox, crockery and kitchen utensils, went over the back fence into the vacant lot. Afterwards the hoboes who camped out in that section prepared their Mulligan stews in unheard-of luxury for months to come. The corrugated-iron garage was moved in one piece a hundred feet away, leaving the Lincoln Continental standing naked in the sunshine. While the top of the house, attic included, along with the old upright piano, Sister Heavenly's throne and souvenir trunk, sailed straight up into the air, and long after the sound of the blast had died away the piano could be heard playing up there all alone.

The outer door of the safe was blown off and went out the

back way along with the kitchen stove. The steel inner door was punctured like a blown-up paper sack hit by a hard fist, and the safe proper went out the front. Scraps of hundred-dollar bills floated in the air like green leaves in a hurricane. Later in the day, people were picking them up as far as ten blocks away and some of the neighbors spent all winter trying to fit the pieces together.

But the floor of the house remained intact. It had been swept clean of every loose scrap, every pin and needle, every particle of dust, but the smooth surface of the wood and linoleum went undamaged.

It was hard to determine afterwards which way Uncle Saint and the nanny goat went, but whichever way they went, they went together, because the two assistants from the Medical Examiner's Office of Bronx County couldn't distinguish the bits of goat meat from the bits of Uncle Saint's meat, which was all there was left for them to work on.

The trouble was, Uncle Saint had never blown a safe before. One-fifth of the nitro would have blown the safe without taking him and the house along with it.

13

Sister Heavenly figured there was more than one way to skin a cat. If Pinky didn't show up soon, she was going to trick Uncle Saint into making like he had found the stuff, and force Pinky to show his hand.

Then she heard the shots. Nothing sounds like pistol shots but pistol shots. She had heard too many of them to be mistaken.

She sat up on the park bench across from Riverside Church and screwed her head around.

Next she heard the screaming.

In the back of her old jaded mind she thought cynically that the sequence was logical – when men shot off pistols, women screamed.

But the front of her mind was alive with conjectures. If anyone else got killed the stuff was going to get so hot it couldn't be touched, she thought.

Then she saw two men come quickly from the apartment house. It was quite a distance to see faces distinctly and both wore their hats pulled low over their eyes, but she knew she'd never forget them.

One was a fat man, definitely fat, with a round greasy face but fair-skinned. His shoulders were broad and he looked as though he might be strong. He wore a dark blue Dacron single-breasted suit. He had the other man by the arm and seemed to be pushing him along.

The other man was thin with a too-white, haggard face and dark circles about his eyes. Even from that distance she made him as a junkie. He wore a light gray summer suit and was shaking as though he had a chill.

They turned and walked quickly in the opposite direction. She saw them get into a Buick Special sedan of ordinary battleship-gray. There was nothing about the car to distinguish it from any car of the same make. From that distance she couldn't read the license number, but the plates were Empire State issue.

She figured she might have something valuable; something she could sell. She didn't know how valuable, but she would wait and see.

She didn't have to wait long. The first of the prowl cars showed up in a little over two minutes. Within five minutes the street was filled with police cars and two ambulances.

By then people were hanging out the windows and the customary crowd had collected. The police had formed lines, keeping the front of the house clear.

She figured it was safe to get closer. She saw a figure on a stretcher brought out and shoved quickly into an ambulance. A third attendant had walked alongside it, holding a bottle of plasma. The siren sounded and the ambulance roared off.

She had recognized the face.

'Grave Digger,' she whispered to herself.

A cold tremor ran down her spine.

Coffin Ed came out walking, assisted by two ambulance attendants whom he was trying to shake off. They managed to get him into the second ambulance and it drove off.

Sister Heavenly was backing off to leave when she heard someone say, 'There's another one, an African with his throat cut.'

She backed away fast. As she was leaving she saw two heavy black sedans filled with plainclothesmen from homicide pull up.

She figured what she had was too damn valuable to sell. It was valuable enough to get her own throat cut.

She walked quickly up the hill to Broadway, looking for a taxicab. She was so disconcerted she forgot to raise her parasol to protect her complexion from the sunshine.

After she had hailed a taxi, got inside and felt it moving, she began to feel secure again. But she knew she had to get rid of Uncle Saint and the red-hot Lincoln, or she was going to find herself up a creek.

When she arrived on the street where she had left her house, she found it filled with fire trucks, police cars, ambulances, and thinly dressed people, for the most part Italians with a sprinkling of Negroes, cooking in the noonday heat, risking sunstroke to satisfy their morbid curiosity.

The whole city was running amok, she thought, from the sugar side to the shabby side.

As the taxi drew nearer, she craned her neck, looking for her house. She didn't see it. From the window of the taxi, looking over the heads of the crowd, she couldn't see the floor that remained. It looked to her as though the entire house had disappeared. The only thing she could see was the Lincoln, standing out like a red thumb in the bright sunshine.

She stopped the taxi before it got too close to the police lines and hailed a passerby.

'What happened down the street?'

'Explosion!' the bareheaded Italian-looking worker gasped, breathing hard as though he couldn't get enough of the hot dusty air into his lungs. 'Blew the house up. Killed the old couple who lived there. Saint Heavenly they were called. No trace of 'em. Musta had a still.'

He didn't pause to see her reaction. He was scrabbling around, like scores of others, picking up scraps of paper.

Well now, ain't that just too beautiful for words? she thought. Then she asked the taxi driver, 'See what that is they're picking up.'

He got out and asked a youth to see a sample. It was the corner of a hundred-dollar bill. He brought it back to show to Sister Heavenly. The youth followed him suspiciously.

'Piece of a C-note,' he said. 'They must have been making counterfeit.'

'That tears it,' Sister Heavenly said.

The two of them stood staring at her.

'Give it back to him and let him go,' she said.

She knew immediately that Uncle Saint had tried to blow her safe. It didn't surprise her. He must have used an atom bomb, she thought. She wished he had picked a better time for the caper.

The taxi driver climbed back into his seat and looked at her with growing suspicion. 'Ain't that the house where you wanted to go?'

'Don't talk foolish, man,' she snapped. 'You see I can't go there 'cause the house ain't there no more.'

'Don't you wanna talk to the cops?' he persisted.

'I just want you to turn around and drive me back to White Plains Road and put me out by the playground.'

At that hour the treeless playground was deserted. The sand-pits baked in the sunshine and heat radiated from the iron slides. The slatted bench on which Sister Heavenly sat burned stripes up and down her backside. But she didn't notice it.

She took out her pipe and filled it with the finely ground stems of marijuana from an oilskin pouch and lit it with an old gold-initialed pipe lighter. Then she opened her black-and-white striped parasol and holding it over her head with her left hand, she held the pipe in her right hand and sucked the sweet pungent marijuana smoke deep into her lungs.

Sister Heavenly was a fatalist. If she had ever read *The Rubáiyát of Omar Khayyám,*, she might have been thinking of the lines:

> The moving finger writes,
> And having writ moves on;
> Nor all your piety nor wit
> Nor all your tears
> Shall cancel half a line of it . . .

But instead she was thinking, Well, I'm back on my bare ass where I started, but I ain't yet flat on my back.

It was life that had taught Sister Heavenly not to cry. A crying whore was a liability; and she had started as a whore. At fifteen she had run away from the sharecropper's shack her family had called home, with a pimp to be a whore because she was too cute and too lazy to hoe the corn and chop the cotton. He had told her that what she had to sell would find buyers when cotton and corn were a drug on the market. The memory brought a smile. He was a half-ass pimp but he was sweet, she thought. But in the end he had kicked her out like the others had afterwards with nothing but the clothes she had on her back.

Then her thoughts turned cynical: Even cotton got rotten with age and corn got too wormy to shuck.

Anyway, after she'd got onto the faith-healing pitch, she had lived high on the hog, which meant she could eat pork chops and pork roasts instead of pig's feet and chitterlings. It had been the other way around after that; she had been the ruler of the roost and had kicked her lovers out when she got tired of them.

She knocked out her pipe and put it away. The ocher-colored pupils of her eyes had become distended with a marbleized effect and pink splotches had formed beneath her leathery skin.

As she walked up White Plains Road the drab-colored

buildings took on blinding bright hues in the sunshine. She hadn't been that high in more than twenty years. Her feet seemed to glide through the air, but she was still in full command of her mind.

She began to suspect she had cased the whole caper wrong from the very beginning. She had figured it as a shipment of H, but maybe it wasn't that at all.

It couldn't be a mother-raping treasure map, she thought with exasperation. That old con game went out when airplanes came in.

Or could it? another part of her mind asked. Could it be that some gang had come up with some treasure somewhere and had made a map of its whereabouts? But what the hell kind of treasure? And how the hell would the map get into the hands of a square like Gus, a simpleminded apartment house janitor?

The weed jag made her thoughts dance like jitterbugs. She turned into a supermarket drugstore and ordered black coffee.

She didn't notice the man next to her until he spoke. 'Are you a model, may I ask?'

She flicked him an absent-minded glance. He looked like a salesman, a house-to-house canvasser type.

'No, I'm one of the devil's mistresses,' she said nastily.

The man reddened. 'Excuse me, I thought maybe you were a model for some advertising agency.' He retired behind a newspaper.

It was the afternoon *Journal American* and she saw the streamer on the page turned toward her:

Two Harlem Detectives Suspended for Brutality

A column was devoted to the story. To one side the pictures of Grave Digger and Coffin Ed looked like pictures of a couple of Harlem muggers taken from the rogues' gallery.

She read as much of the story as she could before the man folded the paper.

So they killed Jake, she thought. In front of Riverside Church.

That must have been when Pinky put in the false fire alarm.

Her thoughts churned furiously. She tried to remember everything Pinky had said, how he had looked and acted. A pattern was beginning to take shape, but the answer eluded her.

Suddenly she jumped to her feet. Her table mate drew back in alarm. But she merely paid her bill and rushed outside and started walking rapidly to the nearest taxi stand.

She looked at her locket-watch when she had paid off the taxi driver in front of Riverside Church. It read 3:37.

She looked up and down the street. The prowl cars had gone and there was no sign left of the police unless it was the black sedan parked down the street from the entrance to the apartment.

She had a sinking sensation in her stomach as the thought occurred to her that it might already be too late.

She opened her parasol and holding it in her left hand and her heavy black beaded bag on her right arm, took hold of her skirt on the right side and, lifting it slightly, sailed down the street and turned into the apartment house.

A big stolid-looking white cop was on guard at the door. He did a double take.

'Hey, whoa there, ma'am,' he said, stopping her. 'You can't go in here.'

On second thought he added, 'Unless you live here.'

'Why not?' she countered. 'Is it quarantined?'

'What do you want in here, if you don't live here?' he reiterated.

'I'm taking up subscriptions for the colored peoples' Old Folks Home,' she said blandly.

But he was a conscientious cop. 'Do you have a license?' he demanded. 'Or at least any identification or something to show who you are?'

She arched her eyebrows. 'Do I need any? After all, I'm a sponsor.'

'Well, you'll have to come back later, I'm afraid. You see, the police are conducting a search in there right now and they don't want any strangers in the house.'

'A search!' she exclaimed, giving the impression of horrified shock. 'For a body buried in the basement?'

The cop grinned. She reminded him of a character out of a stage play he had seen once.

'Well, not exactly a body, but a buried treasure,' he said.

'My land!' she said. 'What's the world coming to?'

His grin widened. 'Ain't it awful?'

She started to turn away. 'Well, if they find it, don't forget the old colored people,' she said.

He laughed out loud. 'Never!' he said.

She went into the next-door apartment house and took up a station in the foyer from which she could watch the entrance next door. Passing tenants looked at her curiously, but she paid them no attention.

One thing was for sure, she was thinking; if it was there, the police would find it. But on the other hand, why hadn't the two gunmen found it, since they would know exactly what they were looking for?

Her head swam with doubts.

I wish to Jesus Christ I knew what the hell I was looking for, she thought.

She saw a small panel truck pull up before the house next door. It had the letters S.P.C.A. painted on the sides.

Now what the hell is this? she thought.

She saw two men wearing heavy leather gloves and long white dusters alight from the compartment and enter the house.

A few minutes later they returned, leading Pinky's dog Sheba by a heavy chain leash.

And all of a sudden it exploded in her head. All this goddamn time wasted! she thought disgustedly. And there it was all the time.

It fitted like white on rice.

She watched the attendants put the dog into the body of the S.P.C.A. truck and drive away. She had to fight back the impulse to rush out and call the bitch by name and claim her. But she knew she'd wind up in the pokey and they'd still have the dog. It was like watching a friend go down in the middle of the sea, she thought. You could feel for him but you couldn't reach him.

She started racking her memory trying to figure out what S.P.C.A. stood for. It couldn't be *Special Police for Collaring Animals*. That didn't make any sense. What would they have special police to collar animals for when any policeman could do it?

Then suddenly she remembered: *Society for the Prevention of Cruelty to Animals*. Where she had heard about it she didn't know, but there it was.

She left her station and walked over to Broadway and entered the first bar. It took a little time to find the telephone number of the Manhattan branch of S.P.C.A.

A woman's pleasant, impersonal voice answered her call.

'I've heard you sell stray dogs,' Sister Heavenly said. 'I'd like to buy a dog.'

'We don't actually sell the stray dogs that are brought in to us,' the woman explained. 'We try to find congenial homes for them where they will fit in with the families, and we ask for a donation of two dollars to help carry on the work of the foundation.'

'Well, that's all right,' Sister Heavenly said. 'I can spare two dollars. Have you got any dogs on hand?'

'Well, yes, but is there any particular kind of dog you would like?'

'I want a big dog. A dog as big as a lion,' Sister Heavenly said.

'We seldom have dogs that size,' the woman said doubtfully. 'And we are very particular about whom we let take them. Could you give me an idea of your reasons for wanting a dog that size?'

'It's like this,' Sister Heavenly said. 'I have a roadhouse in New Jersey. It's not far from Hoboken. And to be frank with you, it's not the most law-abiding place you can find. But there's a big fenced-in yard for the dog to run. And of course there're always plenty of bones, not to mention meat, for him to eat.'

'I see. You need it for a watchdog?'

'Yes. And he can't be too big. Our last watchdog was fairly big. He was a German dog. But prowlers killed him.'

'I see. You say *him*. Does it make any difference if the dog is female?'

'That's all the better. As long as she's big.'

'It so happens that you have called at an opportune time,' the pleasant-voiced woman said. 'There might be a large female dog available within a few days. Would you mind giving me your name and address?'

'A few days!' Sister Heavenly exclaimed, filling her voice with dismay. 'I thought I could get one today. I'm leaving tomorrow on two weeks' vacation and I want to leave the dog there with the caretaker while I'm gone.'

'Oh, that's not possible, you see we have to check . . . But . . . Won't you hold on for a moment, perhaps . . .'

Sister Heavenly held on.

After a time the pleasant voice said, 'Hello, are you there?'

'Yes, I'm still here.'

'Well, it's quite likely that you may get your big dog today just as you wish. It's highly irregular of course, but one has just come in and – if you will call me back an hour from now we will give you a definite answer. Okay?'

'Okay,' Sister Heavenly said and hung up.

She looked at her watch. It read 4:03.

She telephoned back at exactly 5 o'clock.

The pleasant-voiced woman said she was so sorry, but a detective had come and had taken the dog away.

Sister Heavenly knew just how people felt when they said *'Doggone!'*

14

Coffin Ed was in a crying rage, caught up in an impotent self-tormenting fury that gave to his slightly disfigured face a look of ineffable danger.

'These miserable mother-raping crumbs,' he grated through clenched teeth. 'These sonofabitching rathole snakeshit hopped-up sons of syphilitic whores with their doctored rods trying to play tough by shooting an unarmed man in the back. But they ain't seen nothing yet.'

He was talking to himself.

There was an electric clock on the wall at the end of the dazzling white hospital corridor. It read 2:26.

He thought bitterly, Yeah, they suspended us for punching a mother-raping pusher in the guts and ain't three hours passed before some drugged-up killer has got Digger.

Tears were seeping from his eyes and catching in the fine scar ridges between the patches of grafted skin on his face as though his very skin was crying.

Nurses and interns passing down the corridor gave him a wide berth.

What made it all the worse, he felt a sense of guilt. If I hadn't been so mother-raping cute and had listened to Digger and just let it alone until the guys from homicide came he might not have got it, he thought.

Grave Digger lay on the operating table beyond the closed white door. Death wasn't two feet off. He needed blood and they had used the one lone pint of his type blood they had in store. It wasn't enough. The only other place they had it was in the Red Cross blood bank in Brooklyn. A police car led by two motorcycle cops opening up the city traffic was bringing it as fast as anything could possibly move in the big congested town. But time was rapidly running out.

Coffin Ed had just been told he didn't have the type of blood Grave Digger needed.

Now I can't even do this for him, he thought. But one thing is for sure, if he goes down, he ain't going alone.

He had a lump on the side of his head, back of the left ear, as big as a goose egg, and his head seemed split in all directions by a blinding headache that began behind the eyes. The doctors had said he had concussion and had tried to put him to bed. But he had fought them off with a raving scarcely controlled violence and they had gotten the hell away from him.

It was a high-class, well-equipped hospital, the nearest to the scene of the shooting; and he knew if Grave Digger could be saved, they would save him there. But that did nothing to assuage his self-condemning rage.

Down at the end of the corridor he saw his and Grave Digger's wife ascending the head of the stairs. He turned and fled through the first doorway. He found himself in a room for minor surgery. The lights were off and it was temporarily out of use.

He couldn't bear to face Grave Digger's wife and he didn't want to see his own. His daughter was in a summer camp in the Catskills. There was no one to hinder him. Mentally, he thanked someone for this small favor.

The wives were not permitted in the operating room. They stood outside the door in the corridor, their brown faces set like graven images. From time to time Grave Digger's wife touched a handkerchief to her eyes. Neither of them spoke.

Coffin Ed looked for a way to get out. There was a connecting door at the end of the room but it was locked. He raised the bottom half of the frosted-glass window. It opened onto a fire escape. He went outside. A group of medical students in an adjoining building stopped to watch him. He didn't notice them. He went down one story and the swing ladder dropped to the paved driveway that led to the emergency entrance at the rear.

He went out to the street and walked bareheaded in the blinding midday sunshine to where his car was parked on Riverside Drive. Heat shimmered before his vision, distorting his perspective. His head ached like rheumatic fever of the brain.

Half an hour later he pulled into the driveway of his house in Astoria, Long Island. How he managed to get there he never knew.

He had been given a sedative at the hospital to take home. The label on the bottle read: *One teaspoonful every hour.* He tossed it into the trash can outside the kitchen door and let himself into the kitchen.

He put the Silex coffee maker on the gas stove, with enough coffee in it to make mud. While waiting for it to boil he stripped off his clothes and piled them on the chair beside the bed. In the bathroom medicine cabinet he found a bottle of Benzedrine tablets. He took two and drank water from the washbowl faucet in his cupped hand. He heard the coffee maker boiling and went into the kitchen and turned off the fire.

After that he took a shower, turning it from lukewarm to as cold as he could bear. He held his breath and his teeth chattered as the cold needles bit into his skin. His head felt as though sheets of lightning were going off in his brain, but the lethargy left his limbs.

He toweled and went into the bedroom and put on jockey shorts, nylon socks, lightweight black shoes with rubber soles, the pants to his brand-new dark gray summer suit, and a blue oxford cloth shirt with a button-down collar. He omitted the tie. He didn't want anything to be in his way when he reached for the handle of his revolver.

His shoulder holster hung from a hook inside the door of the clothes closet. The special-made, long-barreled, nickel-plated .38-caliber revolver, that had shot its way to fame in Harlem, was in the holster. He took it out, spun the chamber, rapidly ejecting the five brass-jacketed cartridges, and quickly cleaned and oiled it. Then he reloaded it, putting a U.S. army tracer bullet into the last loaded chamber and leaving the one under the trigger empty so there wouldn't be an accident in case he had to club some joker across the head with the butt.

He placed the revolver on the bed and took down the holster. From the shelf in the closet he took a can of seal fat and smeared a thick coating on the inside of the holster. He wiped the excess off with a clean handkerchief, tossed the hankerchief into the soiled-clothes hamper, and strapped on the shoulder sling. When he had cradled the revolver, he strapped a stopwatch to his left wrist.

He chose a knockout sap from the collection in his dresser drawer. It was made of plaited cowhide covering a banana-shaped hunk of soft solder, with a whalebone handle. He stuck this into a hip pocket made especially for that purpose.

He slipped a Boy Scout knife into his left pants pocket. As an afterthought he stuck a thin flat hunting knife with a grooved hard-rubber handle, sheathed in soft pigskin, inside the back of his pants alongside his spinal column, and snapped the sheath to his belt. Not that he thought he would need it, but he didn't want to overlook anything that might keep him living until his job was done.

I'd drink some *everlasting* water if I knew where some was at, he thought grimly.

Then he put on his coat. He had chosen that suit because the coat was bigger than any of his others and it had been tailor-made to accommodate his shoulder sling.

He dropped a new box of cartridges into the leather-lined pocket on the left side, then put a handful of cartridges with tracer bullets into the leather-lined pocket on his right side.

He went into the kitchen and drank two cups of scalding hot, mud-thick coffee. It recoiled in his empty stomach like cold water on a hot stove, but stayed down. The Benzedrine had killed his appetite and left a dry brackish taste in his mouth. He scarcely noticed it.

Just as he was about to leave the house the telephone rang. For a moment he debated whether to ignore it, then went back into the bedroom and picked up the receiver.

'Johnson,' he said.

'This is Captain Brice,' the voice said from the other end. 'Homicide wants you to get in touch – Lieutenant Walsh. And keep out of this. Stay home. Let the men with the shields have it. If you get in any deeper I'm not going to be able to help you.' After a pause he added, 'Nobody is.'

'Yes sir,' Coffin Ed said. 'Lieutenant Walsh.'

'They got the blood from Brooklyn, in case you haven't heard,' the captain added.

Coffin Ed held on to the receiver, but he didn't have the nerve to ask.

'He's still hanging on,' Captain Brice said, as though reading his thought.

'Yes sir,' Coffin Ed said.

The phone began to ring again as soon as he cradled the receiver. He picked it up again.

'Johnson.'

'Ed, this is Lieutenant Anderson.'

'How goes it, Lieutenant?'

'I called to ask you.'

'He's still in there fighting,' Coffin Ed said.

'I'm going over there now,' Anderson said.

'It ain't any use. He don't know anybody yet.'

'Right. I'll wait 'til it's time.' A pause, then, 'Keep out of this, Ed. I know how you feel, but keep out of this. You don't have any authority now and anything you do is going to make it worse.'

'Yes sir.'

'What?' Anderson was startled. Coffin Ed had never said *yes sir* to him before.

But Coffin Ed had hung up.

He telephoned the West Side homicide bureau and asked for Lieutenant Walsh.

'Who's calling?'

'Just tell him Ed Johnson.'

After a while a deliberate, scholarly-sounding voice came on.

'Johnson, I'd like to know what you think about this.'

'Up until we found the African's corpse, I didn't think anything about it. We couldn't figure that from any angle. Then when they got Digger, that changed the story. There must have been two –'

'We know that,' Lieutenant Walsh cut him off. 'Two professional gunmen. We know they were after something. The whole place is being gone over by a crew from the safe and loft squad. But they haven't found anything, or even anything to indicate what they're looking for. What do you think it might be? If we knew that, we might know where to start.'

'I think it might be H; a shipment of H that's taken off.'

'We thought of that. The narcotics squad is working on it. But a shipment of heroin, even as pure as it comes, large enough to induce murder is not easy to hide. A really valuable shipment, considering all the wrappings it would need, would run to about the size of a football. By this time anything that size would have been found by the crew at work on it.'

'It doesn't have to be a shipment. It can be a key.'

'A key. I hadn't thought of that; I don't know about the searchers. Just a key to a plant somewhere. Maybe you're right. I'll pass the suggestion on. Anyway, they're going to keep after it until they're satisfied there's nothing there.'

'If it isn't that I don't know what it is.'

'Right. By the way, what do you think has happened to the janitor and his wife? Gus and Ginny Harris, they are called. And they had a helper, an ex-pug called Pinky.'

'Gus and Ginny were supposed to sail on the *Queen Mary* today and Pinky's on the lam.'

'They had booked passage but they didn't sail. All three of them have just dropped out of sight.'

'They can't stay hidden forever.'

'They can if they're at the bottom of the river.'

Coffin Ed waited. He had said all he had to say.

'That's all for the time, Johnson. Stick around. We might want to get in touch with you again. And Johnson –'

'Yes sir.'

'Keep out of this. Let us handle it. Okay?'

'Yes sir.'

Coffin Ed went into the kitchen and drank a glass of water from the refrigerator bottle. His throat felt bone dry.

Then he went into the garage and put a suit of paint-smeared coveralls into a large canvas bag left behind by the painters who had worked on his house. He put the bag into the back of his car and got in and drove down the street to Grave Digger's house.

He knew the doors would be locked so he walked around to the back and jimmied the kitchen window. His body had a light weightlessness that put an edge on his reflexes, making them a shade too quick. He'd have to be careful, he cautioned himself. He'd kill someone before he knew it.

Two of the neighborhood children, a little boy and girl, stopped playing in the yard next door and looked at him, accusingly.

'You're breaking into Mister Jones's house,' the little boy piped up, then shouted at the top of his voice, 'Mama, there's a burglar breaking into Mister Jones's house.'

A woman came quickly from the back door of the next-door house just as Coffin Ed got one leg over the window ledge.

He nodded toward her and she smiled. They were all colored people on that street and the grownups knew one another; but the children seldom got sight of the detectives, who were sleeping most of the day.

'That's just Mister Jones's partner,' she told the children. 'Mister Jones has been hurt.' She figured that explained it.

Coffin Ed closed and locked the window and went into the bedroom and opened the clothes closet. A long-barreled nickel-plated .38-caliber revolver identical with his own was cradled in a holster hanging from an identical hook inside the door. He slipped it from the holster, spun the cylinder to make certain it was loaded, then stuck the barrel down inside the waistband of his trousers with the handle angled toward the left side.

'Almost ready,' he said out loud, and inside of his splitting head he felt the tension mount.

He went into the living room, searched about in the writing desk, and scribbled on a sheet of stationery: STELLA, *I've taken Digger's gun.* ED.

He brought it back and propped it on top of the dressing table.

He was turning away to leave when a sudden thought struck him. He stepped over to the night table and picked up the telephone and dialed homicide again.

When he got Lieutenant Walsh, he asked, 'What happened to the janitor's dog?'

'Ah yes, she was turned over to the S.P.C.A. Why?'

'I just remembered that it was hurt and I wondered if anybody was taking care of it.'

'That's what I forgot to ask,' Lieutenant Walsh said. 'Do you happen to know how she got that wound in the head?'

'We saw the African take her down toward the river early this morning and then come back without her. That was early this morning – a little after five. We didn't have any reason to be suspicious, so we didn't question him. When we got back to the place around one o'clock she was lying in front of the side gate with that hole in her head.'

'That clears up that,' Walsh said. 'How's Jones coming on?'

'He's still breathing – the last I heard.'

'Right,' Walsh said.

They both hung up at the same instant.

Coffin Ed telephoned the hospital. He identified himself.

'I'm calling to find out how is Detective Jones.'

'His condition is grave,' the impersonal woman's voice replied.

Pain flashed in Coffin Ed's head.

'I know that,' he said through clenched teeth, trying to control his unreasonable rage. 'Is it any graver?'

The impersonal voice thawed slightly. 'He has been placed in an oxygen tent and has passed into a coma. We are doing all we can for him.'

'I know that,' Coffin Ed said. 'Thank you.'

He hung up and went outside through the front door, locking it on the snap latch, and got into his Plymouth sedan.

He stopped in the neighborhood pharmacy to get four and a half pounds of sugar of milk. The pharmacist had only half the amount in supply, so Coffin Ed told him to fill it out with quinine.

The pharmacist stared at him goggle-eyed, torn between suspicion and amazement.

'It's for a gag,' Coffin Ed said. 'I'm playing a joke on a friend.'

'Oh,' the pharmacist said, relaxing, then added with a grin, 'As a matter of fact, this mixture is good for a cold.'

Coffin Ed had him wrap it securely and seal all the seams with Scotch tape.

From there he drove into Brooklyn and stopped in a sporting goods store. He bought a square yard of rubberized silk, in which he carefully wrapped the package from the pharmacy. The clerk assisted. They sealed the seams with rubber cement.

'That'll keep it dry on the bottom of the sea,' the clerk said proudly.

'That's what I want,' Coffin Ed said.

He bought a small blue canvas utility bag and put the package inside of it. Then he bought a pair of dark green goggles and a soft woolen Scotch beret large enough so that it wouldn't press too hard on the knot on his head.

On first glance he looked like a beatnik escaped from Greenwich Village. But that impression was quickly dispelled by the bulge beneath his breast pocket and the frightening tic in his dangerous-looking face.

'Good luck, sir,' the clerk said doubtfully.

'I'll need it,' Coffin Ed said.

15

It was one of those big, old-fashioned, four-story houses on 139th Street between Seventh and Eighth avenues. It had a limestone façade flanked by Ionic columns and a hand-carved mahogany door with crystal-glass panels which had been enameled black. There was a carriage entrance on one side. The carriage house had been converted into a garage.

Years back, when the street had been inhabited by the nouveau riche, it had claimed pretensions. Then during the 1920s a smart colored real estate promoter filled the old mansions with socially ambitious Negro professionals, and it became known throughout the length and breadth of Harlem as 'Strivers' Row.'

But during the depression of the 1930s, hard times came upon the strivers like a storm of locusts and the street went rapidly down from sugar to shucks. The houses were first partitioned into flats, then the flats were divided into rooms. Then the madams took over and filled the rooms with prostitutes.

Coffin Ed parked his Plymouth in front of the house, got out and opened the back door. He reached inside and grasped the handle to a chain and pulled out the oversize dog. She was muzzled again but the wound on her head had been neatly bandaged and she looked more respectable.

He led her around the side of the house, past the carriage entrance, and rang the back doorbell.

The kitchen door was wide open. Only the heavy screen outer door was locked. Coffin Ed watched a fat kimono-clad woman waddle in his direction.

She peered through the screen and said, 'My God, it's Coffin Ed.'

She unlocked the door and opened it for him to enter, then drew back quickly at sight of the dog. 'What's that thing?'

'It's a dog.'

Her eyebrows went up. She had hennaed hair almost the same shade as her eyes, and wrinkled skin which was heavily coated with Max Factor pancake makeup and copper-red suntan powder. She was called Red Marie.

'It won't bite, will it?' she asked. Her voice sounded as though she had something down her throat, and her thickly painted, greasy red lips curled and popped, exposing gold teeth smeared with lipstick.

'It can't bite,' he said, pushing into the kitchen.

It was a modern electrical kitchen. Everything was spotlessly clean and dazzling white. A young whore, still active and competing, dreams of diamonds and furs. But an old whore, no longer active and competing, whether she's gone down to a toothless hag or up to a rich landprop, dreams of a kitchen like this. It contained every kind of electrical gadget imaginable, including a big white enamel electric clock over the stove.

Coffin Ed looked at the clock. It read 4:23. Time was getting short.

On a small white enamel table to one side a white enamel radio stood on top of a blond oak television set. A television program was showing but the sound was turned off.

A big slouchy man with short kinky red hair growing in burs about a bald spot sat in a tubular stainless-steel chair with his elbows propped on top of a large white enamel kitchen table.

'We was just listening to the radio,' he said. 'It said Digger has been shot up and you both is off the force.'

He sounded happy about it; but not happy enough to get his teeth knocked out.

Coffin Ed stood in the center of the floor, holding the dog loosely by the chain.

'Listen,' he said. 'You can make it light on yourselves. I ain't got much time. Where can I find Pinky?' His voice sounded forced, as though he had a stricture in his throat, and the tic was running away.

The man glanced at him, then looked back at the bottle of whiskey before him on the table and reaching out, touched it with the fingertips of both hands.

He had a broad flat face, rough reddish skin and little reddish eyes from which tears leaked continuously. He was called Red Johnny. He might have been related to Pinky.

He wore a white silk shirt open at the throat, green-and-red checked suspenders, tan gabardine pants, white-and-tan wing-tipped shoes, and the usual heavy gold jewelry denoting a successful pimp: gold ring with a huge milky stone of unknown origin, gold ring with three-quarter-carat yellow diamond, and a gold lodge ring with the outline of an owl with two ruby eyes.

He crossed glances with Red Marie, standing to the left and behind Coffin Ed, then he spread his thick-fingered hands and looked at the gun bulge on Coffin Ed's shoulder.

'We're clean,' he muttered. 'We keeps squared off with the captain and you ain't rightly got no authority no more.'

'We don't even know nobody called Pinky,' Red Marie spoke up.

'All you're doing is asking for trouble,' Coffin Ed said. His jaw muscles rippled beneath the tic as he tried to control his rage. 'You ain't got one mother-raping reason on earth to cover for

Pinky. It's just that I'm the law and you resent me. Now you can show it. But you're making a mistake.'

'What mistake?' Red Johnny asked. He could barely keep the insolence from his voice.

'You're over fifty,' Coffin Ed said. 'You spent thirteen years in stir on a second-degree murder rap. Now you're doing all right. You got this house through a lucky hit on the numbers and you set this ex-hustler up as a madam. I know you both. She did her bit too in stir for stabbing a teen-age whore not quite to death. Then when she got back on the bricks she streetwalked for a chickenshit pimp called Dandy who got his throat cut by a square for playing around with the deck in a five-and-ten-cent blackjack game. Now you're both going great. Times are good. Tricks are walking. The streets are full of lains. Squares everywhere. The money's rolling in. You're paying off the man. You're sitting pretty. But you're making one mistake.'

'You said that before. What mistake?'

Coffin Ed let the handle to the dog chain drop to the floor. 'I ain't playing,' he said.

Red Johnny folded his arms and leaned back in his chair. His gaze dropped slightly to the impression of the gun stuck in Coffin Ed's belt.

'Course you ain't rightly got no authority to come in here and ast me no questions 'bout nobody,' he began, and from across the table Red Marie warned, 'Don't push him, Johnny.'

'I ain't pushing him and I ain't going to let him push me neither. I done already told him I don't know no Pinky and he can –'

He never got to say what Coffin Ed could do. One whole side of Coffin Ed's face convulsed in a muscular spasm as his right hand flashed toward his hip. Red Johnny moved out of animal reflex; his head jerked about, eyes following the movement of

Coffin Ed's hand; his left foot braced against the floor; his left arm flew up instinctively to ward off the blow. He didn't see the motion of Coffin Ed's left hand at all as it came from the front with Grave Digger's pistol and smashed the barrel in a back-handed swing straight across his loose-lipped mouth.

The whole front line of Red Johnny's teeth caved into his mouth, two of the bottom teeth flew out sidewise like corn popping, and Red Johnny spun over backward in the tubular chair. The back of his head hit the linoleum floor with a dull thud while at the same instant his feet flew upward and kicked the bottom of the enamel table. The whiskey bottle rose six inches in the air and shattered the drinking glass when it came down.

The abrupt ear-shattering din panicked the dog. She leapt over Red Johnny's face, making for the inner door. Red Johnny thought she was leaping for his throat and tried to scream. Nothing came out but a spray of blood and he choked on his teeth.

Coffin Ed didn't see it. He had swung back to take a left-handed bead on Red Marie's stomach, and had frozen her in midstride, her right hand waving out in front, left hand floating out behind, her big sloppy fat body poised on the ball of her right foot like a rip-roarious burlesque of a ballerina executing a movement in *Swan Lake*.

But no one thought it was funny. Her face was distorted with terror and Coffin Ed looked like a homicidal maniac.

The chair scraped as Red Johnny rolled over, clawing at his throat, making choking sounds.

The inside of Coffin Ed's head was one great flaming-red blast of pain, through which sound trickled like curses. From some-where came the thought that Red Johnny was trying to draw a gun. He wheeled back and kicked Red Johnny on the base of the jaw.

'Ugh!' Red Johnny grunted and fainted.

The dog pushed open the inner door and ran down the hall, her chain clanking behind her.

Red Marie grabbed at the table edge for support; her fingers slipped off and she fell to the floor with a crash.

From the front of the house came the sound of women screaming.

Coffin Ed stood in the center of the floor with the long-barreled nickel-plated pistol in one hand and the sap in the other, looking as dazed as though he had just emerged from a shock treatment for insanity.

On the television screen three shrunken lunatics, arms about one another's shoulders, were dancing frantically back and forth, eyes rolling and lips flapping but no sound coming out.

Coffin Ed's head suddenly cleared; only a shrill, almost imperceptible whistling in both ears still remained.

He pocketed the sap, stuck the pistol back into his belt, and reached down and rolled Red Johnny over onto his stomach.

'Lawd, don't kill him,' Red Marie wailed. 'I'll talk.'

'Give me a tablespoon and shut up,' Coffin Ed grated. 'He'll do his own mother-raping talking.'

She crawled on all fours around the table and got a spoon from the drawer.

'Bring it here,' Coffin Ed said, kneeling beside Red Johnny and lifting his head.

Red Johnny had swallowed his tongue. Coffin Ed stuck the spoon down Red Johnny's throat and kept levering until he got enough tongue out so he could reach in with his other hand and grab hold of the tip. The tongue was so slippery with blood it took half a dozen tries before he got hold of the tip and yanked it back into position. Blood gushed over his hands onto the floor and four broken teeth fell out.

'Here, you hold his tongue down until he gets his breath,' he ordered Red Marie and made her take the handle of the spoon.

He got up and went to the sink and washed the blood from his hands with cold water from the tap, dried them on a kitchen towel. There was a small bloodstain on the cuff of his blue shirt, but he didn't bother about it.

He came back and stood over the two people on the floor. 'I'm going to ask some questions –'

'I'll answer 'em,' Marie said.

'Let him answer them. When the answer is yes, nod your head. You hear me?'

Red Johnny's head nodded carefully.

'When the answer is no, shake your head. And don't make any more mistakes.'

Again Red Johnny nodded.

'It hurts him,' Red Marie said.

'I want it to hurt him,' Coffin Ed said. 'You run a shooting gallery in here?'

Red Johnny nodded.

'It ain't really no regular shooting gallery,' Red Marie said defensively. 'It's just we have some jags here sometimes, just folks with a chicken habit –'

'And pushers,' Coffin Ed cut in.

Red Johnny shook his head.

'If I catch you lying –'

'I hope God may kill me,' Red Marie blurted. 'We don't let no pushers come in here. It's just parties we has and folks bring their own stuff. We gets a few skinpoppers but the H they has ain't even strong enough to be habit-forming. Ain't none of 'em real addicts. Most of 'em just blows weed. Just to get a kick. That ain't our racket. We just sells poontang here.'

'Pinky is an addict.'

'Yes, but –'

'Let him answer.'

Red Johnny nodded.

Coffin Ed stepped back from the pool of blood that was reaching toward his feet.

'Lawd be my secret judge, he don't come here for it,' Red Marie said. 'He don't come for the jags neither. He just buys pussy.'

'Has he got any particular choice?'

'He too ugly to score a home here; he's like Jesus, he loves 'em all.'

'Was he here today?'

Red Johnny shook his head.

'Last night?'

Again Red Johnny shook his head.

'Know where he lives?'

The answer was the same.

'You've been doing so much talking; talk some now,' Coffin Ed said to Marie.

'We don't know nothing 'bout Pinky, I swear 'fore God; he just come here to see the girls and I wish to heaven he had picked on somebody else for that; I don't need his money and I can't stand his looks.'

'Where does he hang out?'

'Hang out?' She started to parry, but one glance at Coffin Ed's face loosened her tongue so that she began to stammer. 'Kid Blackie's gym is all I know. I heered him say once he'd just come from there. You know somewheres else, Johnny?'

Red Johnny shook his head.

'All right,' Coffin Ed said. 'That's Pinky's dog I got. I'm gonna take it through this house and let it sniff around. If I find out you're lying –'

'As God be my benefactor and protector and my haven –' Marie began, but Coffin Ed cut her off.

'You're making me puke. How is it that all you worn-out whores get so chummy with God?'

'It ain't really Him,' Marie said solemnly. 'It's Jesus.'

He couldn't tell whether she was in earnest or not. He pushed open the door and went toward the front hall and called the dog.

'She's here!' a woman's voice replied.

He went up the front stairs to the second floor and traced the voice to an open bedroom at the rear. A brownskin whore in a negligee was stuffing cream chocolates into the side of the dog's mouth through the muzzle. The bitch loved it.

Coffin Ed took the chain leash and led the dog. He didn't know exactly what he was looking for, but he was playing out a hunch. Nothing came of it but some curses from some whores working at their trade.

'Gawddammmm!' one of the girls said disgustedly when her white customer became suddenly deflated at the sight of the big colored man and monstrous dog poking into the room. 'As long as it took to get this slow-John started –'

Upon seeing a pay telephone in the front hall, Coffin Ed stopped and telephoned the hospital.

The answer was the same.

Red Johnny and Red Marie were nowhere in sight when he passed through the kitchen.

He led the dog around on the other side of the table from the pool of blood, through the back door and around the house. He didn't encounter anyone. The whole block looked deserted.

He put the dog in the back of the Plymouth and got into the front seat behind the wheel. He looked at his watch. It read 4:51.

He had a sudden crazy, desperate feeling that he was looking for a needle in a haystack, wasting time; and that time was the most precious thing on earth.

16

Kid Blackie was a short black man with a face like a monkey's and a shining bald head. His torso was naked in the dim-lit stinking heat of the small dirty gym. Big flopping breasts shaped like gourds with rusty-looking teats as big as a woman's hung down to his navel. His flabby muscles seemed about to drop from the bones and his bay window was big enough to give birth to quintuplets.

He had his thumbs hooked in frayed suspenders holding up baggy-seated pants that looked loaded, and was chewing the stub of a cigar in the corner of his mouth, as he watched two young chocolate-skinned middleweights work out on the greasy square of canvas.

'Wait a minute, Ed,' he said and blew on a whistle that hung from a string about his neck.

The boys stopped punching and stared at him.

He climbed into the ring and squared off with one of the boys.

'Like this,' he said, the cigar butt wobbling in the corner of his mouth, and jabbed a left at the boy's face.

When the boy's guard flew up automatically, he crossed a right to the boy's stomach, bringing it down. The boy's right shoulder dropped as he started a looping right hook. Kid Blackie hooked a left to the boy's jaw so fast the boy never saw it. The boy sat down, looking dazed.

Kid Blackie turned to the other boy. 'You seen how I done it?'

The boy nodded mutely.

'You try it.'

The boy jabbed with his left. Kid Blackie went under it and left-hooked him in the stomach. The boy bent in slightly, dropping his left arm, and tried to cross with his right. But he wasn't fast enough. Kid Blackie threw an overhand right to his jaw and knocked him unconscious.

He spat frayed tobacco onto the canvas and climbed down out of the ring. His old glassy brown eyes looked sad.

'These boys that turn up nowadays,' he bemoaned. 'If they was chicks they'd never get hatched.'

Kid Blackie had been lightweight champion of the world at one time. Rumor had it that he had squandered over a million dollars on white women and Cadillacs. He didn't look as though he regretted it.

'All old people say the same thing,' Coffin Ed dissented. 'There're always some good and some bad. You don't expect everybody to be like you.'

'Maybe you're right.' He watched the two boys helping one another up. 'What's on your ass?'

'I'm looking for Pinky.'

Kid Blackie scratched his bald head. 'That's funny. Some bitch was just in here looking for him too. Cat-eyed woman. Ain't been more'n ten minutes ago.'

Coffin Ed tensed and his tic started jumping.

'By herself?'

Kid Blackie wasn't looking directly at him, but he didn't miss the sudden change.

'Yeah,' he said. 'She come up by herself but I got curious. Only reason for a bitch like her be looking for Pinky would be to shoot him, so when she left I looked out the window. She got in a car with two white jokers – looked like mobsters.' He let it go at that.

Coffin Ed felt his heart constrict and his breath turned rock-hard in his lungs. I'm on your tail now, you mother-rapers, he thought. Pain flooded his head like a sudden hemorrhage and his tic went spasmodic. He tried to control his voice.

'Get a look at 'em?'

'Not much. Come on, let's take a gander. Maybe they're still hanging around.'

They walked to the grimy flyspecked window and looked down on 116th Street.

'Had a gray Buick – little one,' Kid Blackie added.

Their gazes searched the parked cars lining the curbs.

The sun was on the south side and the street lay in shadow. Colored people dressed for the heat milled about on the wide sidewalks, shiny black faces peering from beneath a variety of headgear, black arms protruding from light cotton fabrics.

A two-wheel pushcart loaded with slices of watermelon packed in ice and covered with wet gunny sacks was parked behind an empty ice truck. A hand-lettered sign on one side read: SUGAR TOOF GORGIA MELON, with the S turned around. Water dripped from the bottom.

Farther down an old man with a smaller pushcart was selling glasses of flavored ice. The varicolored bottles stood in a rack about a block of ice covered with wet newspaper. Fronting on the sidewalk behind it was an open hot-dog counter with big glass bottles of orange-flavored ice water and a grill covered with franks like soldiers on parade.

Venetian blinds covered the windows of the bars. Signboards in the lobby of a movie theater depicted gangsters never seen on land or sea shooting it out with blasting rods. On the street in front of it, skinny black children wearing loincloths romped in a stream of water gushing from a fire hydrant.

Coffin Ed had left the dog in his Plymouth and she had her head out of the window, panting. A crowd had collected to stare at her. They kept a respectful distance despite her muzzle.

One little boy was holding up his mongrel in his arms to see the big dog. The mongrel didn't like that business.

There was no sign of a gray Buick.

Kid Blackie shook his head. 'They musta gone.'

The distant blaring of a jukebox came from a bar somewhere below. A bottle fly buzzed against the grimy windowpane.

'You didn't get a look at 'em?' Coffin Ed asked finally, trying to keep the disappointment from his voice.

'I didn't see 'em too good,' Kid Blackie confessed. 'The mugs looked like mugs look anywhere. One looked sort of bony, white-faced, like he was sick, a hopheaded-looking character. Other was a fatty, too light to be a greaser, maybe a Swede. Both of 'em was wearing straw hats and smoked glasses. That mean anything to you?'

'They sound like the ones who sapped me and got Digger.'

Kid Blackie clicked his tongue. 'Too bad about Digger. Think he'll make it?'

There wasn't much sympathy in his voice, but Coffin Ed understood it. Kid Blackie liked Digger, but he was so old he was glad it was somebody else dying and not himself.

'Can't tell 'til the deal's down,' he said.

'Wish I could help you. The woman was dressed sharp, had on a light green suit –'

'I know her.'

'Well, that's all I seen.'

'Every little bit helps. You ain't seen Pinky?'

'Not since three days ago. What you think these mobsters want with him?'

'Same as me.'

Kid Blackie looked at Coffin Ed's face through the corners of his eyes and dropped it.

'Too bad about that big ape,' he said. 'He might have made the grade if it wasn't for his skin.'

'What's the matter with his skin?' Coffin Ed asked absently. He was thinking of the janitor's wife, trying to figure this new angle.

'Bruises too easily,' Kid Blackie said. "Touch him with a feather and he'll turn black-and-blue. In the ring it always looks like he's getting beat to death when he ain't even hurt. I remember once the ref stopped the fight and Pinky wasn't even –'

'I ain't got much time, Kid,' Coffin Ed cut him off. 'You got any idea where I can find him?'

Kid Blackie scratched his shiny bald head. 'Well, he's got a pad somewhere on the Riverside Drive.'

'I know that, but he's on the lam.'

'Yeah? In that case I couldn't say.' Kid Blackie screwed up his eyes and gave Coffin Ed a tentative look. 'A man can't ask you no questions, can he?'

'It ain't that,' Coffin Ed said. 'I just ain't got time to answer.'

'Well, I heered he got an aunt up in the Bronx somewheres,' Kid Blackie volunteered. 'Called Sister Heavenly. You ever heered of her?'

Coffin Ed was thinking. 'Yeah, once or twice. But I've never seen her.'

'From the stone age they say. She got a faith healing pitch. Cover-up they say.'

'For what?'

'Pushing H they say.'

Inside of his blinding headache Coffin Ed's thoughts were jumping like ants frying on a red-hot stove. Whichever way it went, it came back to H, he was thinking.

'Has she got a temple?' he asked.

'I couldn't say.' Kid Blackie shook his head. 'Pinky says she's got a pisspot full of money but she wouldn't give him the sweat off her ass. She must got some kind of joint.'

'Know whereabouts it's at?'

'I couldn't say. Somewheres in the sticks.'

'That don't help much. There're sticks all over the Bronx.'

Kid Blackie decided finally to give up on the cigar butt. He spit it to the floor and carefully picked the shreds from his snaggletooth mouth.

'Who might know is Daddy Haddy,' he said. 'You know where he's at?'

'Yeah,' Coffin Ed said, turning about to leave. 'See you.'

'Don't tell him I told you.'

'I won't.'

All the time he was there Kid Blackie had been looking him over covertly. His wise old eyes hadn't missed a thing. He had made the two guns and the sap and he figured they weren't all.

He let Coffin Ed reach the head of the staircase, then called, 'Wait a minute. You got some blood on your shirt cuff.'

He was curious to know whose blood it was but it was too risky to ask outright.

Coffin Ed didn't even look at his cuff; he didn't stop walking; he didn't look around. 'Yeah,' he said. 'And there's going to be some more.'

17

Unlike the opium derivatives and cocaine, marijuana gives one an esoteric appetite.

Sister Heavenly had just come from seeing Daddy Haddy. After listening to Daddy Haddy's recital of Pinky's latest brainstorm, she had a sudden wild craving for something she'd never eaten before. She couldn't even think until she ate; she couldn't figure out what it meant.

Twenty-five minutes later she left her hired car and the driver on 116th Street and staggered up an alley to a small, dirty 'Home-Cooking' restaurant where she knew the cook. It stood in back of a store that advertised: *Seafood – Eggs – Chicken-on-the-Feet – Southern Specialties*. That gave her an idea.

She ordered a half dozen shelled raw oysters, a bottle of sorghum molasses, three raw eggs and a glass of buttermilk.

The big fat black woman who ran the joint had to send next door to fill the order, and she stood over Sister Heavenly and watched her pour sorghum molasses over the oysters and eat them and mix the raw eggs with the buttermilk and drink it.

'Honey, if I didn't know you I'd swear you was knocked up,' she said.

'I ain't knocked up,' Sister Heavenly said. 'But I'm barefooted.' To herself she added, 'And that ain't no lie.'

Suddenly she jumped up and rushed outside in the alley and

was sick. Even the hungry dogs wouldn't touch the mess. She came back and ordered fried chicken.

'Thass more like it,' the big fat cook said.

When Sister Heavenly had finished with the chicken she pushed back her chair and opened her beaded bag below the level of the table to check its contents. Aside from cosmetics it contained a billfold with five one-hundred-dollar bills, three tens and two ones, a handful of loose change rattling around in the bottom, her pipe and pouch of marijuana, a key ring with 13 keys, a .38 Owl's Head revolver with the barrel sawed off to an inch in length and loaded with dumdum bullets, a spring-blade knife with a bone handle, a box of calling cards reading *Sister Heavenly – Healing by Faith*, three lavender initialed linen handkerchiefs, three French teasers that looked like miniature beartooth necklaces, a picture of a slick-haired black man with buck teeth inscribed, *To Choochy from Hoochy*, and an imitation deputy sheriff's badge. 'That don't spell *whore*,' she said bitterly to herself. 'It don't spell nothing.'

She didn't think about Uncle Saint, her blown-up cache or her lost house. She was too old to regret.

It was time that was worrying her now. She knew her time was short. If the devil don't get me, the cops will, she thought. If the cops hadn't already made the hot Lincoln, they would soon. She gave herself until morning. If she hadn't scored by then it would be too late. She couldn't let the sun catch her again in these parts.

After talking to the pleasant-voiced woman at the S.P.C.A. she had figured that the dick who took Pinky's dog was looking for Pinky. She had started looking for Pinky in the hopes of finding the dog.

Her next stop was Kid Blackie's gym.

She had hired an old Mercury sedan driven by a rape-fiend-looking colored man who worked it as a taxi without buying a license. He was a lean, rusty-black, nervous-looking joker with bright red buck-wild eyes. He was a weedhead and she figured she could trust him.

He was drowsing behind the wheel, sucking on a stick of weed, when she came out and got into the back.

'Turn around and go back toward Lenox,' she said. He shifted into gear and executed the U-turn with flourishes like a maestro.

'I know you can drive; you don't have to prove it,' she said cynically.

He grinned at her in the rearview mirror, narrowly missing a woman with a baby buggy crossing the street.

They had got past Eighth Avenue and were headed east when she casually noticed a Plymouth sedan passing on the other side of the street, headed west. At just that moment the dog stuck its head out of the window on her side.

'Sheba!' she screamed. 'Turn around!'

The driver was teaed to the gills and on a livewire edge and her sudden scream scared the living hell out of him. He knew his name wasn't *Sheba* and he didn't know who *Sheba* was. But he figured if *Sheba* was enough to scare the old witch he was chauffeuring about, that was enough for him. He didn't stop to see.

He put his shoulders to the wheel and turned.

Tires squealed. People screamed. Two cars behind him telescoped. A crosstown bus coming from the opposite direction braked so hard it scrambled the passengers into the aisle.

The Mercury lurched and went up over the opposite curb. A sad-looking cripple leaped like a kangaroo through the door of a bar. An old lady was run over by a black-clad preacher shouting, 'Praise God and run for your lives!'

The front bumper knocked over a wooden stand displaying

religious booklets and twenty-four marijuana cigarettes were scattered about the sidewalk.

The driver didn't see a thing. He was standing on the gas and trusting to fate.

'Follow that car!' she screamed.

'What car?' The street was full of cars.

'It turned up Eighth!'

He was already on top of Eighth Avenue, on the inside lane, pushing past 50 miles an hour. But he made another do-or-die turn, going in between a yellow taxi and a cabin truck with not more than a few inches give-or-take each way; tires screaming, drivers cursing. He came into the avenue so fast he almost climbed up in the back seat of a beat-up convertible carrying ten passengers.

The women in the back seat screamed.

Somewhere behind, a police whistle was blowing frantically.

'Don't stop!' Sister Heavenly cried.

'Is I stopping?' he threw over his shoulder as he wrenched the car around the back of the convertible and gave it the gas.

The bug-eyed driver of the convertible looked out from his galaxy of chicks and shouted threateningly, 'Don't you run into my car, nigger!'

But the Mercury was past and closing rapidly in behind Coffin Ed's Plymouth.

'It's the car!' Sister Heavenly hollered. 'Don't get too close.'

'Hell, I gonna pass it,' he said.

Coffin Ed noticed the beat-up Mercury when it passed. At another time he might have taken on the duties of a traffic cop and run it down. But he didn't have the time.

It was just another automobile racer, a black Stirling Moss trying out his car for a 'Grand Prix' somewhere. Harlem was full of 'em. They got teaed on weed and imagined they could drive those old V-8 gas gluttons straight up in the sky, he thought. He noticed that the back seat was empty. He figured some cop up the line would get him if he didn't get himself killed. He put it from his mind.

The Mercury was out of sight when he pulled up before Daddy Haddy's joint.

The little hole-in-the-wall had a red painted front like the big chain of United Tobacco Stores. But Daddy Haddy had named his *Re-United Tobacco Store*; there wasn't anything anybody could do about that.

The shades were drawn.

Coffin Ed glanced at his watch. It read 6:07.

The tenement across the street threw a shadow on the store. But it was too early for it to be closed. Coffin Ed felt his stomach knot.

He got out of his car, walked across the sidewalk and tried the door. It was locked. A sixth sense told him to wipe his prints from the doorknob, get back into his car and drive – he wouldn't get anything here. He was a civilian on a manhunt; he had no authority to investigate what he suspected might reveal a crime; he was outside of the law himself. 'Phone the station, report your suspicions, and let it go at that,' an inner voice told him.

But he couldn't let it go. He was in it; he was committed; he was like the airplane over the middle of the ocean that had passed the point of no return. He thought fleetingly of Grave Digger, but that wouldn't bear thinking about. The pain in his head and the brackish taste in his mouth had become normal, as though he had always had them.

He took a deep breath and looked up and down the street to see if there were any police in sight. He took out his Boy Scout knife, opened the round, needle-point pry, and began fiddling with the Yale lock.

The door had been closed on the latch. Whoever had last left had just pulled it shut. In a moment it was open. He closed and locked it behind him, groped about until he found the light switch, and turned on the light.

There were no surprises.

He found the body of Daddy Haddy behind the glass-enclosed counter. There was a hole in the center of his forehead filled with a glob of blackish blood. It was encircled by powder burns more than an inch in diameter. He put his toe beneath the shoulder and turned the body just enough to see the back of the head. There was a small hard lump at the base of the hairline where the bullet had come out of the skull without force to penetrate the skin and had coursed downward and stopped.

A clean job! he thought without any emotion whatever. No blood. No noise. Someone had held a pistol with a silencer a few inches in front of Daddy Haddy's head and had pulled the trigger. Daddy Haddy had not expected it. So much for that. Daddy Haddy had had it.

The joint had been searched hurriedly but thoroughly. Shelves, drawers, cases, boxes had been turned out, the contents dumped helter-skelter over the floor. Among the unopened packages of cigarettes, scattered cigars, matches, lighters, flints, fluids, pipes and cigarette and cigar holders was a sprinkling of neatly folded decks of heroin and carefully rolled marijuana cigarettes of bomber size. There was still the faint odor of cordite fumes in the hot, close, stinky air.

He waded through the debris and opened the door at the rear. It showed a tiny storeroom containing two padded straight-backed chairs. The air was redolent with marijuana smoke. The treatment was the same.

It was obvious the searchers hadn't found what they were looking for.

Two people already dead. And Digger –? The thought broke

off, then came on again: Small-time dog-ass little Harlem hustlers on the fringe of the narcotics racket. Pee-wee colored scrabblers for a dirty buck. How do they get mixed up in this business? This is mob stuff from downtown. Hired gunmen from a syndicate . . .

He hadn't discovered any lead to Uncle Saint, so he didn't know there were already three others dead from the caper.

He wondered if he oughtn't back out before it got to be more than he could handle. Drop it back into the lap of homicide and the narcotics squad. Let 'em call in the feds.

Then he thought if he reported the crime he'd be detained, held up for hours, questioned. His superiors were going to want to know what he was doing in this business when he had been warned by all of them to keep out.

'They ain't going to like it, Ed.' He didn't realize he had spoken aloud.

But on the other hand, they were going to dig him anyway. He hadn't made any effort at concealment; his prints were every-where. They'd find witnesses to testify he had been there. On one side was the devil, on the other the deep blue sea.

He thought of Grave Digger again. He thought of having to break in a new partner – that is, if he ever got back on the force. He knew the Harlem hoodlums would make life rough with Grave Digger gone. He thought of how Grave Digger had tracked down the hoodlum who had thrown acid in his face; how he had shot him through both eyes. He thought of the effect on the Harlem gunslingers. He knew if he backed down now, he'd never live it down.

There was nothing in there that he found of any use. Nothing he didn't know before he came inside.

I can't find them, so the only thing for me to do now is let 'em find me, he thought and went outside and pulled the door shut behind him.

A little girl about eleven or twelve years old had the back door of his car open and was trying to entice the dog onto the sidewalk. But she was too scared of the dog to reach inside and get the leash. She stood back a distance on the sidewalk and said, 'Here, Sheba. Here, Sheba. Come on, Sheba.'

It struck Coffin Ed as odd that she knew the dog's name but didn't know the dog.

But before his mind had a chance to work on this, he caught a picture from the corners of his eyes that reacted instinctively on his brain. A youth was standing on the other side of Eighth Avenue at the corner of 137th Street looking up at the sky. Coffin Ed knew automatically there wasn't anything in the sky at that moment to attract the attention of a Harlem youth.

'Let her alone,' he told the little girl and closed the car door.

The little girl ran up the street. He didn't give her another thought.

He walked around the car as though he were going to get in behind the wheel. He had the door open. Then he seemed to think of something and closed the door and turned and started to cross Eighth Avenue.

Two cars were coming along the other side and he had to stop and let them pass.

The youth turned and began sauntering slowly up 137th Street toward St Nicholas Avenue as though he didn't have a thing on his mind.

There was a small chain grocery store on the corner. Coffin Ed headed for it. He knew that in his Scotch beret, green goggles and suit with a coat, he didn't look like a Harlem character out shopping for dinner. But it couldn't be helped; it had to appear he was headed for some definite place until he had closed the gap.

The youth walked faster. He was a coal-black boy, wafer thin, with a long egg-shaped head from which fell locks of long straight black hair. He wore a white T-shirt, blue jeans, canvas sneakers and smoked glasses. The only thing to set him apart from other Harlem youths was his watching Coffin Ed. Harlem youths kept the hell away from Coffin Ed.

Going toward St Nicholas Avenue, 137th Street became residential. It was nearing the dinner hour and the smell of cooking seeped into the street and mingled with the smell of heat and motorcar exhaust. Half-clad people lounged in the doorways, sat on the stoops; naked black torsos gleamed in the sunshine on the upper windows; women's long fried hair glistened and grease trickled down their necks.

Anything was welcome that broke the monotony.

When Coffin Ed yelled to the youth, 'Halt!' everyone perked up.

The youth began to run. He kept to the sidewalk, dodging the people in his path.

Coffin Ed drew Grave Digger's pistol from his belt because it hampered his running. But he didn't dare fire the customary warning shot into the air. He couldn't afford to draw the cops. It was the first time he found himself trying to avoid the cops. But it wasn't funny.

He ran in a long-gaited, flat-footed, knee-straining lope, as though his feet were sinking into the concrete. The light rubber-soled shoes helped, but the heavy artillery weighed him down, and each step set off explosions in his head.

The thin agile youth ran in a high-stepping, light-footed, ground-eating sprint, ducking and dodging between the people pouring into the street.

Sides were taken by the enthusiastic spectators.

'Run, buster, run!' some shouted.

'Catch 'im, daddy!' others echoed.

'Look at them niggers picking 'em up and putting 'em down,' a big fat lady crowed jubilantly.

'Dig the canon, Jack!' a weedhead exclaimed as Coffin Ed ran past.

Two jokers jumped from a parked car at the corner of St Nicholas Avenue and split in an effort to catch the fleeing youth. They didn't have anything against him; they just wanted to join in the excitement.

The youth ducked to the right and one of the jokers lunged at him like a baseball catcher trying to stop a wild pitch. The youth bent low and went underneath the outstretched hand, but the other joker stuck out his foot and tripped him.

The youth skidded forward on his hands and elbows, scraping off the skin, and Coffin Ed closed in.

Now the two jokers decided to take the youth's part. They turned toward Coffin Ed grinning confidently and one said in a jocular voice, 'What's the trouble, daddy-o?'

Their eyes popped simultaneously. One saw the nickel-plated revolver and the other saw Coffin Ed's face.

'Great Godamighty, it's Coffin Ed!' the first one whispered.

How the people up and down that noisy street heard him is one of those mysteries. But suddenly everybody started drawing in. The two jokers took off, running in opposite directions.

By the time Coffin Ed had reached down and grabbed the youth by the back of his neck and yanked him to his feet, the street was deserted save for heads peeking furtively around corners.

Coffin Ed took the youth by the arm and turned him around. He found himself looking into a pair of solid black eyes. He had to fight down the impulse to take Grave Digger's pistol and start beating the punk across the head.

'Listen to me, snake-eyes,' he grated in a constricted voice.

'Walk back to the car ahead of me. And if you run this time I'm going to shoot you in the spine.'

The boy walked back in that high-stepping, cloud-treading gait that marijuana gives. Blood was dripping from his skinned elbows. Silence greeted them along the way.

They crossed Eighth Avenue and stopped beside the car. The dog was gone.

'Who got it?' Coffin Ed asked in a voice that seemed to come from a dried-up throat.

The youth glanced at the tic in Coffin Ed's face and said, 'Sister Heavenly.'

'You're sure it wasn't Pinky?'

'Nossuh, 'twere Sister Heavenly.'

'All right, fine, you know the family. Go around and get inside on the front seat and we're going away where we won't be disturbed and talk.'

The youth started to obey but Coffin Ed reached out again and took him by the arm. 'You want to talk, don't you, sonny?'

The youth glanced again at the tic in Coffin Ed's face and choked, 'Yessuh.'

18

'It's here,' Sister Heavenly told her red-eyed chauffeur.

He pulled the Mercury to the curb beside a red-painted fire-plug in front of the Harlem Hospital, cut the motor and reached behind his car for the marijuana butt. There were spaces to park in front and behind.

'Pull away from this fireplug, you lunatic,' Sister Heavenly said. 'You want the cops to nab you?'

'Fireplug?' He turned his head and stared. 'I didn't seen it.'

Nonchalantly he shifted into gear and pulled up a space.

'Watch my dog and don't let nobody steal it,' Sister Heavenly said and got out.

She didn't hear him mutter 'Who'd want it?' She went across the street to a glass-fronted, white-trimmed surgical supply store.

They were getting ready to close but she told the white clerk it was urgent.

She ordered a large package of absorbent cotton, an eight-ounce bottle of chloroform, a scalpel, elbow-length rubber gloves, a full-length rubber apron, a rubber sheet, and a large enamel basin.

'You forgot the forceps,' the clerk said.

'I don't need any forceps,' she said.

The clerk looked her up and down. She was still carrying her parasol along with her beaded bag, but it was closed. He wanted to be sure to remember her in case of an investigation.

'You ought to leave these things to the hospitals,' he said seriously. 'There're hospitals in the city where they'll do it if it's necessary.'

He thought she was planning to perform an abortion. She dug him.

'It's *my* daughter,' she said. 'I'll do it myself.'

He shrugged and wrapped up the bundle. She paid him and left.

When she returned to the Mercury, the dog was whining, either from thirst or hunger. She got in and put the bundle on the floor and stroked the bitch's head. 'It won't be long now,' she said gently.

She had her chauffeur drive her to a fleabag hotel on 125th Street, a block distant from the 125th Street railroad station, and wait for her while she went inside.

A glass-paneled door hanging askew permitted a hazardous entry into a long, narrow hall with a worn-out linoleum floor and peeling wallpaper, smelling of male urine, whore stink, stale vomit and the cheapest of perfume. What was left of the wallpaper was decorated with graffiti that would have embarrassed the peddlers of obscene pictures in Montmartre.

At the back, underneath the staircase, was a scarred wooden counter barricading a padded desk chair behind which hung a letter box holding identical dime store skeleton keys. A hotel bell stood on the counter; above it on the wall was a pushbutton with the legend NIGHT BELL.

No one was in sight.

Sister Heavenly slapped her gloved palm on the hotel bell. No sound came forth. She picked it up and looked underneath. The clapper was missing. She leaned her thumb on the night bell.

Nothing happened. She took the handle of her parasol and banged the side of the hotel bell. It sounded like a fire truck.

A long time later a man emerged from a half-door in the dark recess behind the desk chair. He was a middle-aged brownskin man with a face full of boils, a head full of tetter, and glazed brown eyes. He had a thick, fat, powerful-looking torso; his collarless shirt was open showing a chest covered with thick nappy hair.

He limped forward, his heavy body moving sluggishly, and put his hands on the counter.

'What can I do for you, madame?' he said in the voice of a baritone singer. His diction was good and his enunciation distinct.

Sister Heavenly was past being surprised by anything.

'I want a quiet room with a safe lock,' she said.

'All of our rooms are quiet,' he said. 'And you are as safe here as in the lap of Jesus.'

'You have a vacancy?'

'Yes, madame, we have vacancies all the time.'

'I'll bet you do,' she said. 'Just a minute while I go get my luggage.'

She went out and paid off her chauffeur and took the dog by the leash and her bundle by the string. When she returned, the proprietor was waiting at the foot of the stairs.

He had an atrophied leg, evidently from polio, and he looked like a spider climbing the stairs. Sister Heavenly followed patiently behind him.

From behind a door on the second floor came loud voices raised in argument: 'Who you talking to, you blue-gum nigger!'

'You better shut up, you piss-colored whore . . .'

From behind another came the sound of pots and pans banging around and the smell of boiling ham hocks and cabbage.

From a third the sound of bodies crashing against furniture, objects falling to the floor, feet scuffling, panting grunts and a woman's voice shrilling, 'Just wait 'til I get loose –'

The proprietor limped slowly ahead without giving the slightest notice as though he were stone-deaf.

They ascended slowly to the third floor and he opened a door with one of the ten-cent skeleton keys and said, 'Here you are, madame, the quietest room in the house.'

A window looked down on 125th Street. It was the rush hour. The roar of the traffic poured in. Directly below was a White Rose bar. A jukebox was blasting and the loud strident voice of Screamin' Jay Hawkins was raised in song. From the room next door came the blaring of a radio tuned up so loud the sound was frayed.

The room contained a single bed, straight-backed chair, chest of drawers, six eight-penny nails driven into a board on the inner wall to serve as a clothes closet, a chamber pot, and a washbasin with two taps.

Sister Heavenly went across the room and tried the taps. The cold water ran but the hot water tap was dry.

'Who wants hot water in this weather?' the proprietor said, carefully touching his face with a dirty handkerchief.

'I'll take it,' Sister Heavenly said, tossing her bundle onto the bed.

'That will be three dollars, please,' the proprietor said.

She gave him three dollars in small change.

He thanked her and snapped the inside bolt back and forth suggestively and limped off.

She closed the door, locked it on the inside, and snapped the bolt. Then she laid her bag and parasol on the bed beside the bundle, removed her hat and wig, sat on the side of the bed and took off her shoes and stockings. When she stood up she was baldheaded and barefooted.

The dog began to whine again.

'In just a moment, honey,' she said.

She took out her pipe, loaded it with the finely ground stems of marijuana and lit it with her gold-plated lighter. The dog laid its head in her lap and she stroked it gently as she sucked the smoke deep into her lungs.

Someone knocked on the door and a slick, ingratiating voice said, 'Hey Jack, I hears you, man. Leave me blow a little with you. This is old Playboy.'

Sister Heavenly ignored him. After a while the disgruntled voice said, 'I hopes the man catches you, stingy mother-raper.'

Sister Heavenly finished her pipe and put it away. Then she rolled up her skirt, exposing her thin bird's legs, and pinned it above her knees. She peeled off her silk gloves and put on the rubber ones; and hooked the long rubber apron over her head and fastened it securely behind.

She took the package of cotton, the bottle of chloroform and the chair and sat in front of the open window.

'Here, Sheba,' she called.

The dog came and nuzzled her bare feet. She hooked the handle of the leash onto the lower half of the sash lock, tore off a swab of cotton, saturated it with chloroform and held it to the dog's nose. The dog reared back and broke off the lock. She chased it across the room and stuck the saturated cotton inside the nose of the muzzle. The dog gave a long pitiful howl and broke for the window. She grabbed the end of the chain leash and swung the dog around just before it jumped, then quickly she grabbed the open bottle of chloroform and poured it over the dog's nose. The howling stopped. The dog gasped for breath and settled slowly to the floor, legs extended stiffly front and back. Its lips drew back, exposing clenched teeth, its eyes became fixed; it shuddered violently and lay still.

Quickly she spread the rubber sheet in the center of the floor and placed the enamel basin on it. She dragged the dog and laid its head in the basin and cut its throat with the scalpel. Then she lifted it by the rear legs and let it bleed.

She dumped the blood into the washbasin, turned on the water and left it running. She brought the enamel basin back and began to disembowel the carcass.

It was bloody, dirty, filthy work. She opened the stomach and split the intestines. She was nauseated beyond description. Twice she vomited into the filth. But she kept on.

Down below, the jukebox blasted; next door the radio blared. Strident voices sounded from the street; horns blared in the jammed traffic. Colored people swarmed up and down the sidewalks; the bars were packed; people stood in line in front of the cafeteria across the street.

The hot poisonous air inside of the room, stinking of blood, chloroform and dog-gut, was enough to suffocate the average person. But Sister Heavenly stood it. There wasn't anything she wouldn't do for money.

When finally she had convinced herself there wasn't anything inside of the dog but blood and filth, she threw the scalpel into the carcass and said, 'Well, that's lovely.'

She crawled to the window, put her arms on the ledge, and sucked in the hot, stinking outside air.

Then she stood up, took off the bloody apron and spread it over the bloody carcass, peeled off her gloves and dropped them beside it. The rubber sheet was covered with blood and filth and some had run off onto the linoleum floor.

It ain't any worse than some of the tricks I've turned, she thought.

She went to the basin and washed her hands, arms and feet. She took a fresh handkerchief from her bag, saturated it with

perfume, and wiped her bald head, face, neck and arms, and feet
She remade her face, put on her gray wig and black straw hat,
sat on the bed and put on her shoes and stockings, put down her
skirt, picked up her beaded bag and parasol, and left the room,
locking the door behind her and taking the key along.

The proprietor was coming in from the street as she went out.

'You left your dog,' he said.

'I'm coming back.'

'Will she be quiet while you're gone?'

For the first time in more than thirty years Sister Heavenly
felt slightly hysterical.

'She's the quietest dog in the city,' she said.

19

First, Coffin Ed and the youth called Wop had driven out to the Bronx and looked at the remains of Sister Heavenly's house. A police barricade had been thrown about it and experts from the safe and loft squad were still digging in the wreckage. One look had been enough for Coffin Ed.

Afterwards, employing Wop as his guide, he made a junkie's tour of Harlem. Wop was known to all the landprops as Daddy Haddy's runner and had the entrée. Coffin Ed had the persuader.

Pushing Wop in front of him to ring the doorbells and give the passwords, with the muzzle of Grave Digger's pistol poking in his spine, he had crashed all the notorious shooting galleries in Harlem, the joints where the addicts met to take their kicks and greet their chicks; where the skinpoppers and the schmeckers (those who used the needle and those who sniffed the powder), the pushers and the weedheads gathered for sex circuses and to listen to the real cool jive.

He had gone in with a long nickel-plated revolver in each hand and homicide in his eyes.

He had flushed famous jazzmen, international blues singers, sophisticated socialites both white and colored, prominent people both men and women, mingling with the racketeers and the gamblers, the whores and the thieves and the dregs of humanity;

all being rooked together by the peddlers of the five-colored dreams and the cool dry jags and the hot sex licks.

He had encountered the furtive and the indignant, 'respectable' women who had burst into tears, puffed-up jokers who claimed political pull; those who couldn't care less about being caught and those who figured money would settle it.

His entrance had set off panic, engendered terror, triggered rage. Jokers on the lam had jumped from windows, landprops had threatened to call the police, housewives had hidden under beds, drug-crazed starkers had charged him with stickers.

He had tamed the rambunctious and pacified the pacifists. He was not a narcotics man; he didn't even have a shield. His entrance was illegal and he had no authority. All he had had was muscle, and it hadn't worked.

He had left a trail of hysteria, screaming jeebies, knotty heads and bloody noses. But it hadn't meant a thing. He hadn't gotten any leads, hadn't found out anything he didn't know. Just a blank.

No one had admitted to seeing Pinky all that day. No one had admitted to seeing a yellow-skinned cat-eyed woman in a green suit accompanied by two white mobsters looking for Pinky. No one had ever heard of Sister Heavenly. No one had known anything about anything. He couldn't pull them in and sweat it out.

And yet he knew some of them were lying. He was certain, since talking to Kid Blackie, that Ginny, the janitor's wife, and the two gunmen were making the same tour. They were either in front of him or behind him, or perhaps more than once they had crossed paths. But he hadn't seen a sign of them, nothing to indicate whether they were following him or in front of him. He had doubled back and laid in wait and they hadn't showed.

Now it was eleven o'clock at night. Coffin Ed sat in his parked car with the lights off in the middle of a dark block on St Nicholas

Avenue opposite the park. He could feel the trembling body of the youth beside him, even though they were separated by two feet of space. He could hear Wop's teeth chattering in the dark. The youth's jag had worn off and the smell of terror came from him like a sickening miasma.

Coffin Ed reached into the dark and turned on the dashboard radio to catch the eleven-o'clock news broadcast.

A mealymouthed male voice came on, imitating some big-name newscaster, and blabbed about domestic politics, the Cold War, what the Africans were doing, the latest on the civil rights front and a fistfight between two motion picture actors in El Morocco.

Coffin Ed wasn't listening but the sound of the voice set his teeth on edge. The top of his head felt like it was coming off. He had long since discarded his goggles but his eyes felt gritty.

He tried to think, but his thoughts didn't make any sense. They were jumping about in his head like buck-and-wing dancers on their last breath. 'Give a little, take a little,' one side of his brain was saying, while the other side was cursing in a blinding rage. He thought for a moment of how he would line the mother-rapers up and shoot them down.

He realized that he was wandering badly and caught himself. 'Ain't no time to blow your top now, son,' he told himself.

They had just one more place to go. It was run by a Harlem society matron, and it wasn't going to be easy to crash. He didn't want to hurry it. If it turned out to be another blank, he'd be up shit alley.

'You said you was going to give me my fare to Chicago,' a choked dry voice stammered from the dark beside him.

'You'll get it,' he said absently, his cluttered thoughts echoing, 'He thinks that's far enough.'

'Kin I get some of my clothes?'

'Why not?' he said automatically, but he didn't even hear the question. The thought of Chicago had got mixed up with the two gunmen he was hunting and he added aloud, 'Mother-rapers better get off the face of the earth.'

Wop shrunk into silence.

The voice from the radio blabbed on: '. . . when Queen Elizabeth passed over the bridge . . .' It sounded to Coffin Ed as though he said 'when Queen Elizabeth *pissed* over the bridge . . .' and he wondered vaguely what did she do that for.

'You going to take me by my room?' Wop stammered hesitantly. 'What for?'

'They going be laying for me. They going kill me. You know they going kill me. You promised you'd protect me. You said if I steered you to them cribs wouldn't nobody hurt me. Now you going let 'em –' He began getting hysterical.

Coffin Ed drew back wearily and slapped him across the face.

The voice cut off and the hysteria subsided, followed by snuffling sounds.

Coffin Ed listened to the newscaster report the finding of Daddy Haddy's body by the patrolman on the beat. The words caught in his brain like red-hot rivets: '. . . died of gunshot wounds received earlier today while investigating a homicide in the basement of an apartment house on Riverside Drive. Jones, known locally in Harlem as Grave Digger, was one of the famous Harlem Detective team, Grave Digger Jones and Coffin Ed Johnson. They were on suspension for assaulting an alleged dope peddler named Jake Kubansky who subsequently died. The assailant, or assailants, are unknown. Reports from the homicide bureau –'

He reached out and turned the radio off. It was a reflex action, without thought. Perhaps from a subconscious desire to reject the knowledge by stopping the voice.

His mind fought against acceptance. He sat without moving, without breathing. But finally it sank in.

'That's it,' he said aloud.

Wop hadn't heard a word of it. His terrified thoughts were concentrated on himself.

'But you're going to take me to the station, ain't you? You going get me safe on the train, ain't you?'

Coffin Ed turned his head slowly and looked at him. The muscles of his face were jumping almost out of control, but his reflexes were like a sleepwalker's.

'You're one of them too,' he said in a constricted voice. 'Give you another month or two and you'll be on junk. You'll have the monkey on your back that you got to feed by stealing and robbing and murdering.'

As the voice hammered him with deadly intensity, Wop cringed in the corner of his seat and got smaller and smaller.

'I ain't robbed nobody,' he whimpered. 'I ain't stole nothing. All I done was just work for Daddy Haddy. I ain't hurt nobody.'

'I'm not going to kill you yet,' Coffin Ed said. 'But I'm going to hang on to you, because you're all I got. And you better hope we turn up something at Madame Cushy's if you don't want to get left. Get out.'

Coffin Ed got out on the street side and when he walked around the front of the car he had a sudden feeling that he was being watched from the park. He stepped onto the sidewalk, made a right turn and wheeled about, drawing from the greased holster in the same motion. His gaze raked the sidewalk, flanked by the low stone wall of the park, and above the rocky brush-spotted terrain rising in a steep hill to Hamilton Terrace.

A few scattered couples strolled along the pavement and old people in their shirtsleeves and cotton dresses still occupied the wooden benches. The heat had not let up with the coming of darkness and people were reluctant to turn indoors, but there was no movement within the dangerous confines of the dark grassless park. He saw no one who looked the least bit suspicious.

'I keep feeling ghosts,' he said as he holstered his revolver and pushed Wop before him toward the glass door of the apartment house.

It was an old elevator house, well-kept, and he knew that Madame Cushy lived on the top floor. But the front door was on the latch. His gaze ranged up the list of names above the pushbuttons and settled on one that read: *Dr J. C. Douglas, M.D.*

There was a house intercom beside the row of buttons and when he got the doctor on he said, 'I gotta see you, Doc, I gotta case bad.'

'Let it wait,' the doctor snapped. 'Come in tomorrow morning.'

'Can't wait 'til then. I got a date for tomorrow. It's my money,' he argued roughly.

'Who is this?' the doctor asked.

'Al Thompson,' Coffin Ed said, taking a chance on the name of a pimp.

'I can't cure you overnight, Al,' the doctor said. 'It takes two days at least.'

'Hell, give me all the units at one time, Doc. I been chippie chasing and I'm in trouble. I don't wanna have to kill my whore when she comes back.'

Coffin Ed listened to the doctor's chuckle, and heard him say, 'All right, Al, come on up; we'll see what we can do.'

The latch began to click and Coffin Ed opened the door and pushed Wop into the hall. They rode up to the top floor.

Madame Cushy's was the black enamel door at the front.

'Have you been here before?' Coffin Ed asked Wop.

'Yassuh. Daddy Haddy has sent me with some stuff.' He was trembling as though he were seeing ghosts himself.

'All right, you ring it,' he said.

He flattened himself against the wall while Wop pushed the button.

After a time there was a faint click and a round peephole opened outward. Wop looked at the reflection of his own eye.

'What do you want, boy?' a woman's cross and impatient voice came from within.

'I'se Wop; Daddy Haddy sent me,' he stammered.

'No he didn't, he's dead,' the voice said sharply. 'What are you after?'

Coffin Ed knew he had goofed. He stepped out so he could be seen and said, 'I'm with him.'

He was still wearing his beret and it took a moment for the voice to reply, 'Oh! Edward! Well, what the hell do you want?'

'I want to talk to you.'

'Well, why didn't you ring yourself? You ought to know better than to try to front this punk into my house.'

'I know better now,' he said.

'All right, I will let you in, but not as a cop,' she conceded.

'I've been suspended,' he said. 'Didn't you know?'

'Yes, I know,' she said.

There were two locks on the door, both equipped with adjustable cables to hold it at any position, one near the bottom and one near the top; and they worked so silently the door began to open before he knew she had unlocked it.

'This dirty little boy stays out,' she said.

'He's my mascot.'

She eyed Wop distastefully and stepped back so he wouldn't touch her when he passed.

A wide short entrance hall, flanked by two closed doors, ended at glass double doors of a front lounge and a narrow hallway turned off to the left somewhere. Muted male and female voices, along with the sound of jazz, came from the lounge. There was a faint smell of incense in the overplayed atmosphere of respectability.

After closing and locking the front door she stepped past them and opened the door to the right. Coffin Ed pushed Wop before him into a small sitting room that obviously took turns for other purposes. On one side, behind a glass-topped cocktail table littered with an impressive collection of pornographic picture magazines, was a studio couch equipped with as many odd straps as a torture rack. On the other were two armchairs with suggestive-looking footstools. An air conditioner fitted in the bottom of the window was flanked by a television set and a console radio-phonograph. All manner of obscene figurines filled a three-tiered bookcase in the near corner. Oil nudes of a voluptuous colored woman and a well-equipped colored man faced each other from opposite walls. The air conditioner was turned off and there was the faint sweetish smell of opium in the air.

Madame Cushy followed them in, closed and locked the door, and turned to stare at the demoniacal tic in Coffin Ed's face with impersonal fascination.

She was a buxom Creole-looking mulatto woman with sleepy, brown, bedroom eyes, black hair worn in a bun at the nape of her neck, and a faint black moustache. She wore a red décolleté cotton cocktail dress and high-heeled black net shoes, and her neck, arms and hands gleamed and glittered with jewelry. She looked on the wrong side of forty, but still beautifully preserved and well-sexed. Her voice was a flat contradiction of her looks.

'Well, what is it, Edward? And don't ask me anything about criminals, because I don't know any.'

Coffin Ed said in his constricted voice, 'Just a few questions, and I don't want any mother-raping shit.'

Her face went black with a sudden bloodbursting fury. 'Why, you small-time loudmouthed nigger –' she began, but was cut off by a knock on the door.

A woman's flat unmusical voice from the entrance hall said, 'It's me – Ginny. I may as well go on if you'll let me out.'

'Just a moment, dear,' Madame Cushy forced herself to say, and the next moment she felt her head jerked back by the bun of her hair, a knee in the small of her back, and the sharp edge of a knife blade across her throat.

Coffin Ed had moved so fast during the flicker of her gaze toward the door she hadn't seen it.

'Walk slowly toward the door and open it and tell her to come in,' he whispered in her ear, lowering his knee so she could walk.

She didn't move. Her face was a dull gray-black mask, looking twenty years older than a minute before, and the veins in her temples throbbed like artesian pumps.

'You're going to get yourself killed,' she said in a low tight voice. 'My bodyguard, Spunky, is in the lounge with my husband, and he's wearing a forty-five. There's a sawed-off shotgun in the bureau drawer. And Detective Ramsey is with them, and he's got his police positive.'

'I always thought he was a crooked dick,' Coffin Ed whispered.

'Now you know.'

'But that won't buy you anything. So help me God, I'll cut your mother-raping throat.'

He motioned with his head to Wop to open the door. But Wop was paralyzed with terror. Huge obsidian eyes looked out in a hypnotized stare from a face gone battleship gray.

'I wouldn't do it,' Madame Cushy said.

'Say good-bye,' Coffin Ed said and his arm tightened.

Madame Cushy looked at Wop's eyes. She raised her voice and said, 'Just one moment, Ginny.'

There was the sound of the lounge door opening and a male voice called, 'What is it, baby?' Then it added in a lower tone as though the face had turned away, 'Go see what's happening, Spunky.'

Coffin Ed transferred Madame Cushy's bun from his left hand to his teeth and drew Grave Digger's pistol from his belt while still holding the knife blade to her throat.

When she moved he moved with her, like a monstrous Siamese twin.

Standing behind the door, she opened it and called out, 'It's nothing, dear. I'm trying to fix a rendezvous.' Then in a voice that sounded normal she added, 'Come on in, Ginny.'

Ginny saw Wop's face and hesitated, then stepped inside.

In one continuous motion Coffin Ed kicked the door shut with the edge of his left foot, spun Madame Cushy out of reach, transferred the knife blade to Ginny's throat and closed her mouth with his left forearm, snapping back her head.

She felt the knife blade on her throat, tasted cloth, and saw the huge nickel-plated revolver gripped in a hard black hand just before her eyes. The strength went out of her knees and her body began to sag.

Madame Cushy stepped quickly to the door, opened it and went into the hall. Spunky was a step away, trying to look into the room. She pulled the door shut behind her and said, 'Let them alone for a while.' Then she turned and called through the closed door, 'Call me when you're ready to leave.'

For a moment there was only the sound of their footsteps going toward the lounge and the closing of a door.

Inside the room the sound of Wop's teeth chattering was as loud as castanets.

'Stand up!' Coffin Ed grated in Ginny's ear.

Her knees straightened and she tried to talk. The movement

of her head pressed her long black oily hair into his face.

'Shut up!' he whispered, turning his head to get his face out of the thick, perfumed, rancid, suffocating mass of hair.

The tight, close, abnormal contact of their bodies was aphrodisiacal in a sadistic manner, and both were shaken with an unnatural lust.

'Strip her,' Coffin Ed ordered Wop.

She heard the uncontrollable threads of desire in his voice and thought she was about to be raped. She shook her head and tried again to talk, mumbling what sounded like, 'You don't have to –'

Wop stared in petrified stupidity. 'Strip her?' he echoed as though he didn't understand the words.

'Take her mother-raping clothes off,' Coffin Ed said through clenched teeth. 'Ain't you never done that?'

Wop moved toward her as though she were a lioness with cubs. She was passive, raising each foot in turn for him to remove her shoes and stockings. No one spoke. Only their heavy breathing and the chattering of Wop's teeth were audible. But he took so long to remove her green gabardine suit and chartreuse underclothes the silence became excruciating.

When she was stark naked, Coffin Ed released her.

She turned and saw him for the first time. 'Oh, it's you!' she said in her jarring voice.

'It's me all right.'

She dropped to her knees and clasped his thighs in a tight embrace. 'Just don't hurt me,' she said.

'What the hell!' he said, and grabbed a fistful of her hair and dragged her onto the couch.

Her thick cushiony mouth opened in pain as she sucked in breath, but she didn't dare scream. He rolled her over and carefully examined her for needle marks, but didn't find any.

'Tie her down,' he ordered Wop.

Wop moved like a robot, joints stiff and eyes senseless.

When he had finished, Coffin Ed said, 'Get her compact from her handbag.' Then he leaned over and took her by the hair again. Pulling her head back until her throat was taut, he cut the skin in a thin line six inches across her throat.

She didn't move, didn't breathe. Her eyes were limpid pools of terror set in a fixed stare.

'Give me the mirror,' he said.

He held it before her eyes. 'See your throat.'

A thin line of blood showed where he had cut. She fainted.

He tossed away the compact and said with a choked impotent fury, 'Let anybody's blood flow but their own!'

Then he slapped her until she came to.

He knew that he had gone beyond the line; that he had gone outside of human restraint; he knew that what he was doing was unforgivable. But he didn't want any more lies.

She lay rigid, looking at him with hate and fear.

'Next time I'll cut it to the bone,' he said.

A shudder ran over her body as though a foot had stepped on her grave.

'All right, I'll tell you,' she said. 'I'll tell you how to get it. It's what you want, isn't it?'

He looked at her without answering.

'We'll split it,' she went on. 'We'll cut your partner in too. There's enough for all three of us. You don't want me but you can have me too. You'll want me when you've had me. You won't be able to get enough of me. I can make you scream with joy. I can do it in ways you never dreamed of. You're cops. You'll be safe. They can't hurt you. You can kill them.'

He was caught for a moment in a hurt as terrible as any he had ever known. 'Is everybody crooked on this mother-raping earth?' It came like a cry of agony torn out of him.

Then he said in a voice so tight it was barely audible, 'You think because I'm a cop I've got a price. But you're making a mistake. You've got only one thing I want. The truth. You're going to give me that. Or I'm going to fix you so that no man will ever want anything else you got to give. And I ain't playing.'

'They'll kill me.'

'They're going to kill you anyway if I don't kill them first.'

Twenty-three minutes later he had her story. He had no way of knowing whether it was true. Only time would tell.

He looked at his watch. It read 11:57.

He untied her and told her to get up and dress.

He figured he knew as much as he was ever going to know. Before the payoff, anyway. If what she said was true, he had cased it right himself. If it wasn't true, they were all going down together.

While she was dressing he listened to the sound of a recording coming from the lounge. Other recordings had been playing before, but he hadn't heard them.

It was a saxophone solo by Lester Young. He didn't recognize the tune, but it had the 'Pres' treatment. His stomach tightened. It was like listening to someone laughing their way toward death. It was laughter dripping wet with tears. Colored people's laughter.

His thoughts took him back to the late 1930s – the 'depression' years. When he and Digger had attended a P.S. on 112th Street. They'd heard Lester playing with the Count Basie group at the Apollo, swapping fours and eights with Herschel Evans on their tenor horns.

Pres! He was the greatest, he thought.

'I'm ready,' Ginny said.

'Open the door and call Madame Cushy,' he said.

When Madame Cushy entered the room, he looked her over carefully. Satisfied she was unarmed, he said to Ginny, 'You go out first, I'll follow you,' and then to Wop, 'You come behind me and if you see anybody with a gun, just scream.'

Madame Cushy's lips curled. 'If we were going to hurt you, you'd be dead by now. You won't be hurt around here.'

Silently he sheathed the knife and stuck Grave Digger's pistol back inside his waistband. He looked at her again. 'Digger's dead,' he said, then added, 'And you're living.'

He motioned with his hand and they left in single file.

Madame Cushy held the door open. When Coffin Ed passed her, she said quietly, 'I won't forget you.'

He didn't answer.

He smelled the stink of terror coming from their bodies as they descended in the elevator. He thought bitterly, They're all scared as hell when it's their own lives they're playing around with.

Before crossing the sidewalk to his car, he stood for a moment in the doorway, casing the street, his gun in his hand. He didn't expect any gunplay. If what she had said was true, the gunmen would not be in sight. It was just a precaution. He had learned the hard way not to believe anybody entirely when it's your own life at stake.

He didn't see anyone or anything that looked suspicious.

They walked to the car in the same position as they had left the flat. He got into the front seat from the inside and slid over. The other two came in after him, Ginny in the middle and Wop on the outside.

I wish Digger was here, he thought without thinking.

He didn't think that thought anymore.

20

It took only seven minutes to get there and he didn't hurry. The hurry was off.

He made a U-turn on St Nicholas Avenue, went down the incline to 125th Street, and turned west toward the Hudson River.

For a couple of blocks more, 125th Street was still in the colored section: jukeboxes blared from the neon-lighted bars, loudmouthed people milled up and down the sidewalks, shrill-voiced pansies crowded in front of the Down Beat where the dusky-skinned female impersonators held forth, weedheads jabbered and gesticulated in front of Pop's Billiards Parlor. And then the big new housing project loomed dark and silent.

He turned south on Broadway, west again on 124th Street, and climbed the steep hill of Clermont Avenue behind the high stone wall of International House. Another turn toward the river and he came out into the quiet confines of Riverside Drive beside Riverside Church.

He had kept an eye on the rearview mirror but had seen no indications that he was being followed.

So far so good, he thought.

He parked directly in front of the apartment house and doused his lights; but he sat for a moment casing the street before alighting. Everything looked normal. Nothing was moving for the moment but the cool breeze coming up from the river. Cars parked for the night lined the inside curb despite a city ordinance forbidding it. Nevertheless he had his pistol in his hand when he got out on the street side and walked around the front of the car.

Wop was already getting out on his side and Ginny followed. They crossed the sidewalk in single file and she unlocked the apartment house door with her own key.

Coffin Ed let them both precede him, then said, 'Wait here.'

He went down the hall to the elevator door and brought the elevator to the ground floor. He opened the door and looked inside of it, then closed the door to the elevator itself and stood for a moment studying the outside door to the elevator shaft. There was nothing to be seen. The floor of the elevator was flush with the floor of the hall and the top of the elevator door was flush with the top of the door to the shaft.

He came back and said, 'All right, let's go down,' leading the way.

They came out in the basement corridor and found the night lights turned on as was customary. Coffin Ed stopped them for a moment and made them stand still while he listened. He could see the doors to the janitor's suite, the toolroom, the staircase, the elevator and the laundry, and the one at the back which opened onto the back court. There was not a sound to be heard, not even from outside. His gaze lit for a moment on a short ladder hanging from the inside wall beneath a fire extinguisher. It must have been there before but he hadn't noticed it.

At the end of the corridor, toward the janitor's door, the cheap worn luggage, trunks and household furnishings of the new janitor were stacked against the wall. But the janitor hadn't moved in. There was a police seal on the janitor's door.

Coffin Ed opened his Boy Scout knife and broke the seal. Ginny unlocked the door, stepped inside and switched on the light.

She drew back and cried out, 'God in heaven, what happened?'

It looked the same as when Coffin Ed had seen it last, except the corpse of the African had been removed.

'Your friend got his throat cut,' he said.

She stared in horror at the patches and clots of black dried blood and began trembling violently. Wop's teeth began to chatter again.

'What the hell you so horrified about? It ain't your blood,' Coffin Ed said bitterly, including them both.

Ginny began turning green. He didn't want her sick so he said quickly, 'Just get me the keys.'

She had to pass through the room to the kitchen. She skirted the edge, bracing herself with her hand against the wall, as though traversing the deck of a ship in a storm.

When she returned with the ring of house keys, Coffin Ed said to Wop, 'You stay here.'

Wop looked at the dried blood and the wreckage and turned a shade of light gray that seemed impossible for a person with black skin.

'Do I got to?' he stammered.

'Either that or go home.'

He stayed.

Coffin Ed pushed Ginny into the corridor, closed and locked the door on Wop, then went and bolted the back door that opened onto the rear court. Ginny stood beside the elevator door as though she were afraid to move.

'Stay put,' Coffin Ed directed when he returned and got into the elevator.

Her face broke out in alarm. 'You're not going to leave me here?'

'No worry,' he said and shut the door in her face.

He heard her protesting as he took the elevator up to the first floor but he paid it no attention.

He left the elevator and started down the stairs and ran head-on into Ginny as she was coming up.

'Whoa, where you going, baby?' he said, heading her off.

'If you think I'm gonna –' she began, but he interrupted, taking her arm:

'You're going to show me how to cut off the power to this thing.'

'Awright, awright, you don't have to be so mother-raping rough every time you open yo' mouth,' she grumbled but she obeyed readily enough.

She showed him a small square key on the ring which opened the basement door to the elevator shaft. The power switch was inside. 'Just push it,' she said.

He found a button switch and pushed it.

'Anyway, it's not in there,' she said. 'They said they looked in there.' Her voice wasn't loud, but it wasn't lowered.

He looked into a pit of blackness. 'Shut up and give me a light,' he said.

'There's a light inside. Feel down below and you'll find the switch.'

He groped in the dark and found a small switch. A naked bulb at the end of an extension cord lying on the oil-covered floor lit up showing a six-foot concrete pit at the bottom of the shaft.

A heavy spring bumper supporting a thick steel block rose from the center of the pit. In the back were the cable pulleys and the large electric motor that operated the lift cable. Beside it were a switchboard and adjustment levers.

He lowered himself into the pit, found some greasy cotton waste, and wiped off the instruction plates on the motor and above the levers. One of the levers worked with the motion of a jack handle and was used to jack the elevator up or down to make it flush with the corridor floors.

He jacked it down as far as it would go, about three feet. Then he climbed out of the pit and, leaving the light on, closed the door to the shaft.

He turned the power back on and brought the elevator down to the basement. Now when he opened the door the floor of the elevator was three feet below the floor of the basement. It was now possible to crawl on top of the elevator from the door of the elevator shaft.

He took the ladder from the wall, propped it against the front of the elevator, and climbed up.

'Do you see it?' she asked breathlessly.

He didn't answer.

He put his head and shoulders through the opening atop the elevator, ascended the ladder as far as he could, then wriggled forward on his belly.

'Have you found it?' she called anxiously.

'Pipe down,' he said, feeling about for the blue canvas utility bag.

When he found it he drew it forward beside his hip, then turned over on his back and drew both revolvers. He checked them in the dim, reflected light coming up the sides of the elevator from the pit. They checked.

He began worming forward on his back, inch by inch, moving the bag forward with his elbow.

'It's not there?' she asked. Her voice was strained to the breaking point and jarred on his nerves.

'Will you shut up and let me look!' he grated.

He kept inching forward until his feet touched the ladder. Only his head and shoulders and his hands holding the revolvers remained unseen. Then he knocked the bag out onto the basement floor.

'He's got it!' she screamed, and dove into the elevator.

There was a slight grunting sound as Coffin Ed jumped and came down like a cat somersaulting in the air.

Simultaneously the hophead gunman leaped into the corridor from the staircase.

Both shot before their feet touched the floor. Coffin Ed shot left-handed with Grave Digger's pistol, shooting from the hip in a manner he despised. The gunman shot right-handed with the silenced derringer across his left shoulder, the police positive dangling from his left hand.

In the tight narrow corridor the very air exploded with the hard heavy thunderclap of the long-barreled .38 revolver, drowning the slight deadly cough of the silenced derringer.

The brass-nosed .38 slug hit the gunman on the pivot of the jaw and scattered bone, blood and teeth into the air, while the .44 slug from the derringer burned a hole through Coffin Ed's left sleeve and seared his flesh like a branding iron.

Landing wide-legged and flat-footed in a half-crouch, Coffin Ed pumped two more slugs into the gunman's body, propelling it into a macabre dance before the fat gunman had cleared the bottom step.

Trying to brake his charge and shoot at the same time, the fat gunman threw two wild shots with his .38 automatic, chipping plaster from the ceiling and puncturing the fire extinguisher; while Coffin Ed blasted with both guns and put two slugs side by side in his bulging belly.

Then Coffin Ed's beret sailed from his head in a forward flight like a missile taking off, and a fraction of a second later a brass-jacketed .45 slug coming from behind hit him on the shoulder blade and knocked him flat on his face.

The third gunman had stepped from the laundry, blasting with a .45-caliber Colt army automatic. But before he could squeeze the trigger for the third time, plainclothes dicks poured out of the very walls and crevices, and the corridor erupted with the heavy artillery-like booming of several police positives fired in unison. The gunman went down riddled with thirteen slugs.

It was all over in twenty-seven seconds.

The air was blue-gray and suffocating from cordite fumes, and gun-roar still echoed in their ears.

Two gunmen lay dead on the floor. With his guts perforated, his liver punctured and his spleen blown open, the fat gunman lay dying. A detective was trying to get a statement but he wasn't talking.

Another detective dragged Ginny from the elevator and slipped on the cuffs while a third brought Wop from the janitor's flat. There were nine detectives in all, three from the homicide bureau, three from the narcotics squad and three T-men.

Coffin Ed was gritting his teeth in an agony of bone hurt and trying to push to his feet with his left hand. Two detectives helped him up while another went to the telephone at the end of the corridor and called the precinct station for two police hearses and two ambulances.

'I'm all right,' Coffin Ed said. 'Where's my gun?'

He still had Grave Digger's pistol in his left hand, but he'd been knocked loose from his own by the impact of the .45 slug.

With a grin, a T-man opened his coat and put the pistol into its holster. Coffin Ed stuck the other one back into his waistband. The T-man buttoned the bottom of Coffin Ed's jacket and made a sling for his arm.

The lieutenant from the narcotics squad weighed the blue canvas bag in his hand and looked at Coffin Ed questioningly.

But it was the lieutenant from homicide who asked the question, 'How did you figure it was there?'

The narcotics lieutenant said, 'He didn't. Don't you think we looked there?'

'The hell I didn't,' Coffin Ed said. 'I put it there the first thing I did this afternoon when I left the house.'

'So it's just bait.'

'Yeah. It was the best I could think of.'

For a moment everyone looked at him. His jerking, ugly patchwork face was such a picture of agony, they looked away.

'It gives me an idea,' one of the T-men said. 'If it worked once, it might work twice. We got Benny Mason and his chauffeur staked out down the street, beyond Grant's Tomb. He's watching the entrance here through night field glasses.'

'She said he'd be around somewhere,' Coffin Ed said, nodding toward the woman.

'What's your idea?' the narcotics lieutenant asked.

'Let's send this woman down the street, the other way, carrying this bag. He'll try to get it –'

'Then what? There's nothing in it,' the homicide lieutenant said. 'Nothing to make a charge.'

The T-man smiled. 'We'll put something in it. We were thinking of a trap too, in case we found a way to spring it. So we brought along a little package too, with two kilos of pure heroin. We'll just slip that into the bag –'

'And let him get it?'

'That's the idea. We don't want to disappoint Mister Mason.'

'You'd better hurry,' the homicide lieutenant said. 'In two minutes' time this street will be overrun with prowl cars.'

'That won't make much difference to Mister Mason, as hot as he is after this stuff, but we'll hurry anyway.'

Another T-man produced the package of heroin and they made the substitution and took the handcuffs from Ginny's wrists.

'I won't do it,' she said.

All of them stared at her with those blank looks policemen have when a prisoner defies them.

'What do you have on her?' the T-man asked.

'Conspiracy,' Coffin Ed said.

'We got more than that,' the homicide lieutenant said with a straight face. 'She killed the African.'

'I didn't!' she screamed. 'It's a mother-raping lie!'

'We can prove it,' the homicide lieutenant said in a flat voice.

'You're trying to frame me,' she accused.

'That's the general idea. Of course you can take your chances in court.'

'Dirty mother-rapers!' she fumed.

'Give me thirty seconds alone with her,' Coffin Ed said.

She flicked one glance at his face and her defiance wilted. 'All right, give me the mother-raping bag,' she said.

21

Shadows were framed in dark open windows and the faint distant sound of a siren floated in the silent night when she stepped outside, but no one was in sight.

She turned toward downtown, in the direction of Riverside Church, and began walking fast. She carried the bag as far as possible away from contact with her own flesh, as though it contained a germ bomb that might leak.

Four blocks north, where the drive bends around the sloping green park surrounding Grant's Tomb, a long black Mark II Lincoln, with only its parking lights burning, pulled from the curb. No light emanated from the instrument panel. Only the vague silhouettes of two black-hatted men on the front seat were visible in the dim light coming from the street. The dark aquiline features of the man beside the driver were further obscured by heavy sunglasses. The driver's face was but a round white blur beneath his black chauffeur's cap.

The Lincoln accelerated with incredible speed, but slowed down almost instantly as a prowl car screamed around the far corner by Riverside Church on two wheels, its red light blinking like the eye of hell.

Ginny had seen the Lincoln move and now she welcomed the prowl car as a savior and hastened in its direction. But it was still some distance away. She had started to break into a run when a voice called from the dark entrance of the apartment house next door.

'Honey,' the cracked voice called sweetly.

Her scalp crawled as her head jerked around. Her eyes probed the darkness. She halted on the balls of her feet.

'It's me, Sister Heavenly,' the cracked saccharine voice identified itself.

She stood suspended in flight. 'What the hell do you want?' she demanded viciously.

The prowl car roared past, lighting them briefly with the red spotlight, and dragged to a screaming stop beyond the next-door entrance. It had ignored them.

'Come here, honey, I got something for you,' Sister Heavenly said in what she thought was a sweet cajoling voice.

Ginny realized instantly that Sister Heavenly was after the canvas bag. And I'll give her the mother-raping bag, she decided evilly.

She turned quickly and stepped forward into the dark entrance.

'Here,' Sister Heavenly said sweetly, and plunged the long sharp blade of her knife deep into Ginny's heart.

Ginny slumped without a sound, without so much as a gasp, and Sister Heavenly clutched the bag from her nerveless fingers and hastened down the sidewalk in the same direction.

It went so fast it looked like magic. One moment a young woman in a green suit was carrying a blue canvas bag down the sidewalk; the next moment an old woman in a long black dress and a black straw hat was carrying the same bag in the same direction.

The detectives watching from a black Chrysler sedan parked at the curb up the street didn't know what to make of it.

But Benny Mason's chauffeur said, 'Look, there's been a switch.'

Benny already had his field glasses focused on the bag. 'She gave it to somebody else, that's all,' he said.

The two prowl car cops hit the pavement and charged into the apartment house, obscuring the vision of the watching detectives. For a moment the street looked clear of cops.

The Lincoln accelerated. Behind it the black Chrysler sedan pulled out from the curb. Far ahead down Riverside Drive was the distant red eye of another prowl car coming fast. And from all directions came the sound of sirens, shattering the night, as unseen cars and ambulances converged on the scene.

'Pull over fast,' Benny said.

The Lincoln lunged to the other side of the street and braked silently just ahead of Sister Heavenly and the driver jumped to the sidewalk with a heavy black sap in his hand.

Sister Heavenly saw the car brake and the man jump out in the same sidewise glance. She was carrying the blue canvas bag along with her own black beaded bag in her left hand. Somewhere along the way she had discarded the parasol and instead was carrying the .38-caliber Owl's Head with the sawed-off barrel wrapped in a black scarf in her right hand.

Without turning her body or slackening her pace, she raised the pistol and pumped four dumdum bullets into the chauffeur's body.

'Jesus Christ!' Benny said, and in a fast smooth motion drew his own P38 Walther automatic and shot twice through the open car door.

One slug caught Sister Heavenly in the left side below the ribs and lodged in the side of her spine; the other went wild. She fell sidewise to the pavement and was powerless to move, but her mind was still active and her vision was clear. She saw Benny Mason slide quickly across the seat, leap to the sidewalk, and aim the pistol at her head.

Well now, ain't this lovely? she thought just before the bullet entered her brain.

Benny Mason snatched the bag from her limp hand and jumped back into the Lincoln beneath the wheel. All around him were the red lights of prowl cars converging in the street. His mind was shattered by the head-splitting screaming of sirens. He couldn't see; the air looked red and his brains seemed to be pouring out of his ears. He began accelerating before closing the car door.

The Lincoln crashed broadside into the Chrysler sedan that had cut across in front of it. T-men poured from the Chrysler and surrounded him. He grabbed the bag and tried to throw it, but a T-man reaching through the open door caught him by the wrist and froze the bag in his hand.

'Son, you're going on a long journey,' the T-man said.

'I want to see my lawyer,' Benny Mason said.

The apartment house basement was filling up with uniformed prowl car cops who couldn't find anything to do.

Coffin Ed had his coat off and his right hand held between the buttons of his shirt in place of a sling. Detectives had cut out the back of his shirt and were using a wad of clean pocket handkerchief to staunch the flow of blood until the ambulance arrived. But he was slowly turning gray from loss of blood.

No one knew what the outcome was outside, and the homicide lieutenant put off interrogating Coffin Ed until his wound had been treated. So they were all just standing about.

But Coffin Ed had a need to talk.

'You guys figured too they'd come back?'

'We didn't figure it,' the homicide lieutenant said. 'We engineered it. We knew you were on the prowl and that they were on your tail. That might have kept up all night. So we had to get you here. We knew they'd come after you, just like you did.'

'You got me here? How was that?'

The homicide lieutenant reddened. 'You know by now that Grave Digger is alive?'

Coffin Ed became rigid. 'Alive? The radio said –'

'That was how we did it. We gave out the story. We knew that after you had heard it you would get them here some way to kill them. You're not sore, are you?'

'Alive!' Coffin Ed hadn't heard the rest of it. Tears were streaming unashamedly from his blood-red eyes. He shook his head. 'Well, I'll be a monkey's uncle.' It felt as though his brains were banging against his skull. But he didn't mind. 'Then he'll never die,' he said.

The lieutenant patted his good shoulder as delicately as though it were made of chocolate icing. 'Only way we could figure to cover you. We don't want to lose our good men.' He smiled a little. 'Of course we didn't expect a theatrical production.'

Coffin Ed grinned. 'I dig you, Jack,' he said. 'But sometimes these minstrel shows play on when grand opera folds.'

Then suddenly and unexpectedly he fainted.

22

It was past two o'clock in the morning. The prowl cars and ambulances and hearses had gone from the street and only the black inconspicuous sedans of the plainclothesmen remained among the sedate automobiles of the residents. Quiet once again prevailed in this exclusive residential street.

The crew from the Medical Examiner's Office had been and gone and the six corpses had been taken to the morgue. The fat gunman had died before they arrived and had been tagged D.O.A with the others. He had died without talking. Now there were only the gobs and patches of clotted blood to mark the spots where the six lives had taken exit.

Wop was in jail, safe at last.

But there was still activity in the basement of the apartment house where the interrogations continued and the reports of this fantastic caper were being recorded to shock and horrify what one must hope will be a less violent posterity.

The dining table from the janitor's flat had been set up in the corridor and the two lieutenants and chief of the T-men were sitting in bloodstained chairs about it. A police stenographer sat apart, taking down the words as they were spoken.

Coffin Ed sat facing his interrogators across the table. He had been taken to the Polytechnical Clinic in midtown to have the bullet removed from his shoulder blade and the wound dressed.

His guns, sap and hunting knife had been taken from him by the homicide lieutenant and a detective had accompanied him to the clinic. Technically, he was under arrest for homicide and was being held for the magistrate's court later that morning.

The hospital doctors had tried to put him to bed, but he had insisted on returning to the scene. In lieu of his bloodstained shirt he now wore a hospital nightshirt tucked into his pants, and his arm was in a black cotton sling. Bandages made a lump on his right shoulder like a deformity.

'It's been a bloody harvest,' the T-man said.

'Gun-killing is the twentieth-century plague,' the homicide lieutenant said.

'Let's get to the story,' the narcotics lieutenant said impatiently. 'This business is not finished yet.'

'All right, Ed, let's hear your side,' the homicide lieutenant said.

'I'll start with the janitor's wife, and just repeat what she told me. You have my statement from before. Maybe you can fit it all together.'

'All right, shoot.'

'According to her, all she knew at first was that Gus had disappeared. He left her and the African in the flat at about eleven-thirty and said he'd be back in an hour. He didn't come back –'

'Where was Pinky during this time?'

'She said she hadn't seen Pinky since late afternoon and hadn't thought about him until we questioned her after the false fire alarm.'

'So he wasn't around?'

'He could have been. She just didn't see him. When she found out he was on the lam and Gus hadn't come back, she began to worry about what to do with the dog. They weren't taking the dog and Gus hadn't made any arrangements for it, and she didn't know about S.P.C.A. And of course if Pinky turned up, there was the rap against him for the false fire alarm, and she intended phoning the police and having him arrested. So along toward morning she sent the African out to drown the dog in the river.

'Digger and I were sitting outside in the old struggle buggy when the African took it away. We thought then he might have drowned it, but it was none of our business and we didn't see anything else suspicious, so we left. If we'd stayed twenty minutes longer we'd have seen Sister Heavenly when she arrived.

'She got here about ten minutes to six and said she was looking for Gus. Ginny, that's the janitor's wife, was suspicious – said she was, anyway – but she couldn't get any more out of Sister Heavenly. Then at six o'clock the front doorbell rang. Ginny had no idea who it was, but suddenly Sister Heavenly drew a pistol from her bag and covered her and the African and ordered her to push the buzzer to release the front door latch; and she made them both keep still. Evidently she expected the caller to come straight to the flat. But instead they took away the trunk and left without knocking. When she finally looked out here in the hall and saw the trunk was gone, she ran out of the house without saying a word. And that was the last Ginny saw of her – so she said.'

'What happened to the trunk finally?' the homicide lieutenant asked.

'She claimed she never found out.'

'All right, we'll get on to the trunk tomorrow.'

'I'm in the dark here,' the T-man said. 'Who was going where?'

'She and Gus – he was the janitor – were going to Ghana. They'd bought a cocoa plantation from the African.'

The T-man whistled. 'Where'd they get that kind of money?'

'She told us – Digger and me – that his first wife died and left him a tobacco farm in North Carolina, and he sold it.'

'We have all that from your first statement,' the homicide lieutenant said impatiently. 'Where did the African fit into this caper?'

'He didn't. He was an innocent bystander. When Gus didn't show up after the trunk was taken, Ginny began getting more and more worried. So the African left the house about a half hour after Sister Heavenly to look for Gus. In the meantime it was getting late and Ginny began to dress. They had to go to the dock to get their luggage on board.'

'The trunk should have been delivered the day before,' the T-man said.

'Yeah, but she didn't know that. All that was worrying her was Gus's continued absence. She was just hoping the African would find him in time for them to make the boat. She never saw the African again. She had just finished dressing when the two white gunmen who shuttled her about Harlem first turned up. They said Gus had sent them to take her to the dock. She left a note for the African telling him where she was going. Then the gunmen picked up her luggage and took her out to their car. When they got in the fat man drove and the hophead sat in the back and covered her with the derringer. He told her Gus was in trouble and they were taking her to see him.'

'Didn't she wonder about the gun?'

'She said she thought they were detectives.'

The homicide lieutenant reddened.

'They took her to a walkup apartment on West 10th Street in the Village, near the railroad tracks, and bound and gagged her and tied her to the bed. First they went through her luggage. Then they took off the gag and asked her what she had done with the junk. She didn't know what they were talking about. They gagged her again and began torturing her.'

Abruptly the atmosphere changed. Faces took on those bleak

expressions of men who come suddenly upon an inhumanity not reckoned for.

'Gentle hearts!' the T-man said.

'The next time they took off her gag she blabbed for her life,' Coffin Ed said. 'She told them Gus had pawned the stuff but when she saw that wasn't the answer she said he took it to Chicago to sell. That must have convinced them she really didn't know about it. One of them went into another room and made a telephone call – to Benny Mason, I suppose – and when he came back they gagged her again and left. I figure they came straight up here and searched the flat.'

'And killed the African.'

'I don't think they killed him then. The way I figure it they must have searched twice. In the meantime they probably went and had a talk with their boss.'

'No doubt he sent them back and told them to find it or else,' the narcotics lieutenant said. 'If it was two kilos of heroin it was worth a lot of money.'

'Yeah. I figure the African must have been here when they returned, or else he came in while they were searching. We'll never know.'

'You think they tried to make him talk?'

'Who knows? Anyway, that's when we ran into them and set off the big chase. If I'd listened to Digger's advice and just laid dead, maybe we'd have never tumbled to the dope angle.'

'Not necessarily,' the narcotics lieutenant said. 'We knew a shipment of H had left France, but we didn't know how or when. The French lost it somewhere between Marseille and Le Havre.'

'But we've been on to it for the past week,' the T-man said. 'Working with the local squad – secretly. We've had the waterfront covered from end to end.'

'Yeah, but you'll find out later you didn't cover it far enough,'

Coffin Ed said. 'When the hoods returned to the flat in the Village, Benny Mason went with them. The woman became hysterical when they took off the gag. She said Benny sat beside her and comforted her. He sent out for a doctor who came and treated her and put her under sedation –'

'What doctor?'

'She didn't say and I didn't ask her. Benny sent the doctor away and promised her she wouldn't be hurt again if she was cooperative. Anyway, he won her confidence. In the meantime he sent the hoods out of the room and pulled up a chair, straddled it and sat facing her. And he leveled with her –'

'Then he intended to have her killed,' the narcotics lieutenant said.

'Yeah, but she was too square to dig it. Anyway, he told her that he was the boss of the narcotics racket, that he had the shit smuggled into the country and he had used Gus to pick it up sometimes; and that was how Gus got the money to buy this farm in Ghana. That shocked her; she had believed Gus's hype about his wife leaving him a farm down South. He must have figured it would have that effect because he wanted her to start thinking and remember something she hadn't thought was important before. He went on to tell her that he had had Gus thoroughly investigated and he was certain Gus was a square, just greedy for some money. She agreed to that but she didn't know what he was leading to. He told her that Gus had picked up a shipment of heroin at midnight, worth more than a million dollars, and he was supposed to pass it on in the trunk that was picked up at six o'clock.'

'Picked up from who?' the narcotics lieutenant asked.

'He said the heroin was smuggled into the country on a French liner.'

'We know the French liner that docked this week,' the narcotics lieutenant said. 'We've had it under a tight surveillance.'

'Yeah, but you missed the connection. It was dropped over-board to a small motorboat that passed under the bow without stopping at about eleven o'clock night before last.'

'My men were watching that boat through night glasses and there was nothing dropped overboard,' the T-man said.

'Maybe it was already in the water. I'm just repeating what she said Benny told her. Benny had sent a map to Gus by Jake, the pusher – the one Digger and me got suspended for slugging.'

The city detectives looked embarrassed but the T-men missed the connotation.

'The map showed Gus the exact spot where the shipment would be dropped – only a short walk from here. The boat came up the river and delivered the shipment without ever stopping. Benny said he knew that Gus collected it because the connection told him that Gus was waiting when the boat arrived; and further-more, when the boat returned to the yacht basin in Hoboken the T-men were waiting for it and searched it and they found it clean.'

'By God, I got a report on that boat!' the T-man said. 'It's owned by a taxicab driver named Skelley. He does night fishing.' He turned to one of his men in the background. 'Have Skelley and everyone connected with him picked up.'

The agent went toward the telephone.

'Benny said when his men picked up the trunk the shipment wasn't in it,' Coffin Ed continued. 'She thought maybe Gus had run off with it since it was worth so much. He had gone out before midnight and she hadn't seen or heard of him since, and that wasn't like Gus; he didn't have any friends he could put up with and he didn't have anywhere else to go. Benny said no, he had probably been robbed. They had found Gus and he was hurt and wasn't able to talk and he figured someone had hijacked the shipment –'

'But he left the bundle with Gus for six hours before he sent to pick it up. You think he was that stupid?'

'It was as safe with Gus as anywhere – in fact safer. They had him covered. And since he was actually supposed to sail that day, they figured the trunk dodge would attract less attention than any other. Besides, Benny wasn't taking any chances; he had a lookout posted outside all night. The lookout saw Gus come into the apartment after he had kept the rendezvous and he didn't see anyone leave after then who was carrying anything in which the shipment could have been concealed. The lookout saw Digger and me come and go after the false fire alarm; he saw the African go out with the dog and return without it; he saw Sister Heavenly when she came and left. No, Benny was certain that the shipment hadn't left this house.'

The detectives exchanged glances.

'Then it's still here,' the homicide lieutenant said.

'That's impossible, the way this place has been searched, unless one of the tenants is in on the deal, and we've checked them going and coming and I'd bet my job they're innocent,' the narcotics lieutenant said. 'I personally was with the searching crew when they went through every trunk, every box, every piece of furniture in the storage room; they turned the toolroom inside out, took apart the oil burner, dismantled the washing machines, raked out the incinerator, looked into the sewers, even took two stored automobile tires off the rims; and you saw how the janitor's flat has been searched. We'd have found a signet ring if we'd been looking for it.'

'That's the way Benny figured it. It was too big a bundle to hide, and the only way Gus could have got rid of it was to give it to somebody in this house to hold for him.'

'How big a bundle was it, or did he say?' the T-man asked.

'He told her there were five kilos of eighty-two percent pure heroin in it.'

A cacophony of whistling sounded spontaneously.

'That's one hell of a load,' the homicide lieutenant said.

Calculating rapidly, the T-man said, 'He pays about fifteen thousand dollars per kilo for the junk. Say around seventy-five thousand for the shipment. And after he cuts it down with lactose to about two percent pure, he can retail it for around a half a million dollars a kilo. Say, give or take a little, it's worth two and a half million dollars on the retail market.'

'Now we've got the motive for this massacre,' the homicide lietuenant said.

'But where did the junk disappear to?' the narcotics lieutenant echoed.

'That's the question Benny asked. But she couldn't help him. She said Gus wasn't on good terms with any of the tenants; in fact his relations were on the bad side.'

'No wonder,' the narcotics lieutenant said. 'He didn't need this job.'

'Then Benny asked her about Pinky. She told him all she knew but he wasn't interested in Pinky's life. He wanted to know if Pinky could have got the stuff from Gus and hidden it somewhere in the house. She said he'd have to wait until Gus could talk and ask him, she hadn't seen either him or Pinky since before midnight. Then he confessed that when they didn't find the shipment in the trunk they had killed Gus and thrown his body in the river.'

'That sounds to me like he was lying,' the T-man said, and turned to the narcotics lieutenant. 'Do you believe that?'

'Hell no! They wouldn't kill Gus, even by accident, as long as the five-kilo bundle of H was missing.'

'That's the way I see it.'

'But where is Gus?'

'Who knows?'

'Maybe he's still somewhere in the house,' the homicide lieutenant ventured.

'No, he's not,' the narcotics lieutenant stated flatly.

'Then maybe Benny was leveling with her.'

'No, he was probably trying to scare her,' the homicide lieutenant said.

'He scared her all right,' Coffin Ed said. 'But right away he offered her five thousand dollars if she would help them find him – Pinky that is.'

'Generous bastard,' the T-man said.

'That's when she got on their side,' Coffin Ed said. 'With Gus dead and five G's in her apron, and now the farm was hers too, she could marry the African. She didn't know he was dead. So she put her mind to it, and then she remembered noticing the night before that the trunk had been moved from the storage room into the hall. And as a rule Pinky did all the heavy moving. So she said maybe Pinky had it with him.

'But Benny discarded that too. He had investigated Pinky along with Gus, and he had him cased as a pure halfwit, incapable of handling that much H; he wouldn't know what to do with it. She argued that Pinky had the habit and maybe he took it for personal use. But Benny's lookout had seen Pinky leave here when he went to put in the false fire alarm, and he couldn't have concealed a handkerchief in the ragged clothes he was wearing. And he hasn't been back here since.

'Then she remembered Sister Heavenly's visit. She told him that Sister Heavenly was Pinky's aunt, and that she sold decks of heroin under the guise of a faith healing racket. Then Benny remembered his lookout reporting that Sister Heavenly had left here shortly after the trunk was picked up. He conceded that maybe she was right, maybe Sister Heavenly was the connection, and maybe Pinky had hijacked the bundle. That would be just like a halfwit.

'They took her down to the car and all of them drove up to the Bronx to look for Sister Heavenly. But by the time they got there the house had been blown up and Sister Heavenly had disappeared. But they found out about Uncle Saint and they saw the Lincoln. It was one of Benny's guards whom Uncle Saint had shot over by the French Line dock and they began putting two and two together.'

'We made a line on that,' the homicide lieutenant said. 'We tied it all together after Sister Heavenly's body was identified by the boy, Wop. And we already had a report on the car from an officer stationed at the Lincoln Tunnel.'

'Yeah. Well, they figured Sister Heavenly had already gotten the bundle and had blown up the house to kill Uncle Saint and destroy her tracks –'

'It was just the old joker trying to crack her safe,' the homicide lieutenant said drily. 'The experts made it.'

'Yeah, it wasn't long before they dug that too. Benny had kept lookouts on this house all day, and one of them remembered Sister Heavenly nosing around here after Digger was shot. So Benny figured by that she hadn't made the connection. After then they concentrated on finding Pinky.'

'We kept a line on all of you after that,' the homicide lieutenant said. 'No need of going into detail now.'

'There's just one question I'd like to ask,' the T-man said. 'How was it they didn't spot you, Ed, when you planted your bag on top the elevator?'

'They saw me all right, but they didn't make me. You see, I didn't come in here. I went to the second house from here and went up to the roof and crossed over. I dropped the bag from the top access to the elevator shaft. Besides which I was wearing painter's coveralls and carrying the small bag inside of a large paint-smeared bag the last painters had left in my house. And when I went back outside the same house I'd entered, I was carrying the same big bag.'

'All that is well and good and you deserve credit for it,' the narcotics lieutenant said. 'But where in the hell is the junk?'

The T-man said to Coffin Ed, 'You're the only one here who knew Pinky. Do you think he's capable of that?'

'I wouldn't know,' Coffin Ed said. 'I figure him for a halfwit too. But so was Al Capone.'

'All that this proves is one thing,' the narcotics lieutenant said. 'That this case is not finished; not by a damn sight. Not with a fortune in heroin floating around.'

'For us it's just begun,' the T-man said.

'I've got a hunch we'll find it,' Coffin Ed said.

'A hunch? What hunch?' the homicide lieutenant asked.

'If I told you, you'd laugh.'

'Laugh!' the homicide lieutenant exploded angrily. 'Laugh! With eleven people whom we know of already dead from this one caper, and five kilos of pure poison loose in New York City, and we haven't even scratched the bottom of it. Laugh? What the hell's the matter with you? What's your hunch? Let's hear it.'

'I've got a hunch that Gus is coming back and then we'll find out where it's at.'

In the dead silence which followed, the detectives could feel their hackles rise. They stared at him with blank, deadpan expressions.

Finally the T-man said, 'Well, at least no one is laughing.'

23

The dick stationed on the front door came in and said, 'A Railway Express truck just pulled up out front. I think they're delivering something here.'

'Get back and keep out of sight,' the homicide lieutenant said quickly.

'If it's what I think, we ought to clean up here,' Coffin Ed said.

The detectives looked at him curiously, but they did as he suggested. Quickly they moved the table and chairs back into the janitor's flat and then split into two groups. Some remained there and the others rushed to the other end of the corridor and stationed themselves in the laundry.

Ears were pressed to the closed doors, listening for footsteps. But after the faint sounds made by the opening and closing of the front door, the silence was prolonged.

Then they heard a faint rap on the basement floor, followed by a slight scraping sound as though some small object had been place there stealthily.

Doors were flung open and detectives rushed into the corridor with drawn pistols. They stopped in their tracks as though they had all run into an invisible wall.

A black giant, so black he looked dark purple in the bright light, the blackest man any of them had ever seen, crouched over a large green steamer trunk that hadn't been there before.

It was the giant who inspired their first amazement. He was dressed in the kind of uniform the Railway Expressmen wear, but it was so small on him the coat wouldn't button, the sleeves ended halfway down the forearms and the pants halfway up the legs. His purple-black feet were encased in blue canvas sneakers, and a uniform cap sat atop kinky hair that was decidedly purple.

Pink eyes darted this way and that from the black-purple face. And then the giant started to run.

'Halt!' several voices cried in unison.

But it was Coffin Ed who stopped him by shouting, 'Give up, Pinky. We got you.'

'Pinky!' the homicide lieutenant exclaimed. 'My God, is this Pinky?'

'He's dyed himself,' Coffin Ed said. 'He's really an albino.'

'Now I've seen everything,' the T-man said.

'Not yet,' Coffin Ed said.

The detectives surrounded Pinky and the homicide lieutenant snapped on the handcuffs.

'Now we'll get to the bottom of this,' he said.

'Let's open the trunk first,' Coffin Ed said. 'Give us the key, Pinky.'

'I ain't got it,' Pinky whined. 'The African's got it.'

'All right, let's break it open.'

A dick got a crowbar from the toolroom and pried open the lock.

When they lifted the lid only a jumble of soiled laundry was at first visible. But after pulling it aside, a corpse was revealed. It was the corpse of a small gray-haired man with a small wrinkled black intelligent-looking face. He wore a suit of spotless clean blue denim coveralls and black hip boots.

Everyone began talking at once.

'It's Gus,' Coffin Ed said.

'His neck's been broken,' the T-man said.

'This makes twelve,' the homicide lieutenant said.

'Maybe the bundle is underneath,' a dick said.

'Don't be silly, Benny Mason's had this trunk,' the narcotics lieutenant said.

'Is this your hunch?' the homicide lieutenant asked Coffin Ed.

'More or less.'

'How did you figure it?'

'You'll see.'

The homicide lieutenant addressed Pinky. 'Why did you kill him?'

'I din kill 'im,' Pinky denied in his high whining voice. 'The African and that woman killed 'im.'

'Why did you bring him back here?' Coffin Ed said.

'So they'd be punished, thass why,' he whined. 'They killed my pa and they got to be punished.'

Coffin Ed turned to the homicide lieutenant. 'That's how I dug it. Why would he put in that false fire alarm if he even knew about the H? He just wants to get Gus's wife and the African charged with murder.'

'They done it,' Pinky insisted. 'I know they done it.'

'Let's skip that for a moment,' the homicide lieutenant said. 'The question is where did you find the trunk?'

'At the dock, where they took it. They was going to take him on the ship and throw him in the ocean so nobody'd ever know what happened to him. But I done beat 'em to him.'

'That's a cunning lick,' the homicide lieutenant said. 'When Benny saw there was only a corpse inside, he had it delivered to the wharf.'

'Let's first find out what he did with the junk,' the T-man said impatiently. 'Every minute counts on that angle.'

'We ought to get to that slowly,' Coffin Ed suggested.

'The African and the woman are dead, Pinky,' the homicide lieutenant said quietly. 'And we know they didn't do it. So that only leaves you.'

'Dead? Is they both dead? Sure enough dead?'

'Dead and gone,' Coffin Ed said.

'So you may as well tell us why you did it,' the homicide lieutenant said.

Pinky looked at the corpse for the first time and tears welled in his pink eyes.

'I didn't go to do it. I didn't go to do it, Pa,' he addressed the corpse.

He looked up first at the homicide lieutenant, then at the circle of blank white faces. Then his gaze came to a rest on the ugly brown face of Coffin Ed. 'He was going 'way to Africa and he wouldn't take me with him. I ast him and I begged him. He was going take that yellow woman and he wouldn't take me, and I'se his real 'dopted son.'

'So you killed him.'

'I din go to kill him. But he made me so mad. I ast him again just 'fore he went out fishing –'

'Fishing?'

Everyone became suddenly alert.

'What time was that?' the homicide lieutenant asked.

''Bout half past 'leven. He put on his high boots and got his line and net and went eel fishing. Thass what made me so mad. He'd ruther go eel fishing in the black dark than lissen to me. So I waited and when he come back I ast him again. And he tole me to go away and leave him alone. He say he was too busy to lissen to foolishness.'

'Had he caught any eels?'

'He caught five big black eels. I don't know how he done it so fast but he had 'em in his fishnet. He must 'ave caught 'em before and left 'em in the river 'cause they was all stone dead.'

'How big were they?'

'Big eels. 'Bout two – three pounds, I reckon.'

'Eel skins stuffed with heroin. Waterproof. That's a clever dodge,' the T-man said. 'Only a Frenchman would think of it.'

'What was he doing when you talked to him the last time?' the homicide lieutenant kept hammering gently.

'He were looking in his trunk for somepin. He had it open looking in and I ast him once more to take me with him and he tole me to get the hell away from him. I just 'tended to shake him a little and make him lissen and 'fore I knowed it his neck broked.'

'And you put his body in the trunk and covered it with soiled clothes from the laundry and brought it out here in the hall, then you went and put in the false fire alarm so you could accuse his wife and the African of his murder.'

'They was guilty in they heart,' Pinky said. 'They was going to kill 'im for his treasure map if it weren't for the accident. I heered 'em say they was going to kill 'im. I swear 'fore God.'

'Map! You knew about the map?'

'I seen it just 'fore he went fishing. He tole me it showed where a big mess of treasure was buried in Africa and made me promise not to tell nobody 'bout it.'

The detectives looked at one another.

'Did his wife and the African know about it?' the homicide lieutenant asked.

'Must 'ave. Thass why they was going to kill 'im.'

The homicide lieutenant turned to Coffin Ed. 'Do you believe that?'

'No, he's making it up to justify something.'

'Let's get back to the eels,' the T-man put in. 'Now just where were the eels when you talked to him, Pinky?'

'They were on the floor 'side the trunk where he drop 'em when he come in.'

'What did you do with them?'

'I figure if I left 'em there somebody'd know he'd done already come back from fishing.'

'Yes, yes. But what did you do with them?'

'Them dead eels? I just threw 'em away.'

'Yes-yes-yes; but threw them away where?'

'Where? I just threw 'em in the 'cinerator. It was full of paper and trash and I just threw 'em in there and set it on fire.'

The T-man became hysterical and had to be beat on the back. 'A three-million-dollar fire!' Tears streamed from his eyes.

Pinky stared at him. 'They weren't nothing but stone-dead eels,' he whined. 'They didn't even look fit to eat.'

The detectives roared with laughter as though that was the funniest thing they had ever heard.

Pinky looked as though his feelings were hurt.

Coffin Ed asked curiously, 'Why wouldn't he take you to Africa with him, Pinky? Was it because of your habit?'

'Twarn't 'cause of my habit. He didn't mind that. He said I was too white. He said all them black Africans wouldn't like colored people white as I is, and they'd kill me.'

'I wonder what the court is going to make of that?' the homicide lieutenant said.

24

Charges were dismissed against Coffin Ed.

After coming from the magistrate's court, he and his wife stopped by the hospital to see Grave Digger. He was out of danger, but he was resting and couldn't be seen.

Leaving the hospital they ran into Lieutenant Anderson, who was on his way to see Grave Digger too.

They told him how he was, and the three of them went to a little French bar over on Broadway in the French section.

Coffin Ed had a couple of cognacs to keep down his high blood pressure. His wife looked at him indulgently. She settled for a Dubonnet while Anderson had a couple of Pernods to keep Coffin Ed company.

Coffin Ed said, 'What hurts me most about this business is the attitude of the public toward cops like me and Digger. Folks just don't want to believe that what we're trying to do is make a decent peaceful city for people to live in, and we're going about it the best way we know how. People think we enjoy being tough, shooting people and knocking them in the head.'

His wife patted the back of his big callused hand. 'Don't worry about what people think. Just keep on doing the best you can.'

To change the subject, Anderson said encouragingly, 'It's

going to mean something to the commissioner that you helped clean up this case.'

'The thing I'm happiest about,' Coffin Ed said, 'is that Digger is still alive.'

PENGUIN MODERN CLASSICS

A RAGE IN HARLEM
CHESTER HIMES

'The greatest find in American crime fiction since Raymond Chandler' *Sunday Times*

Jackson's woman has found him a foolproof way to make money – a technique for turning ten dollar bills into hundreds. But when the scheme somehow fails, Jackson is left broke, wanted by the police and desperately racing to get back both his money and his loving Imabelle.

The first of Chester Himes's novels featuring the hardboiled Harlem detectives Coffin Ed Johnson and Grave Digger Jones, *A Rage in Harlem* has swagger, brutal humour, lurid violence, a hearse loaded with gold and a conman dressed as a Sister of Mercy.

With a new Introduction by Luc Sante

'He belongs with those great demented realists . . . whose writing pitilessly exposes the ridiculousness of the human condition' Will Self

Contemporary ... Provocative ... Outrageous ...
Prophetic ... Groundbreaking ... Funny ... Disturbing ...
Different ... Moving ... Revolutionary ... Inspiring ...
Subversive ... Life-changing ...

What makes a modern classic?

At Penguin Classics our mission has always been to make the best books ever written available to everyone. And that also means constantly redefining and refreshing exactly what makes a 'classic'. That's where Modern Classics come in. Since 1961 they have been an organic, ever-growing and ever-evolving list of books from the last hundred (or so) years that we believe will continue to be read over and over again.

They could be books that have inspired political dissent, such as *Animal Farm*. Some, like *Lolita* or *A Clockwork Orange*, may have caused shock and outrage. Many have led to great films, from *In Cold Blood* to *One Flew Over the Cuckoo's Nest*. They have broken down barriers – whether social, sexual, or, in the case of *Ulysses*, the boundaries of language itself. And they might – like *Goldfinger* or *Scoop* – just be pure classic escapism. Whatever the reason, Penguin Modern Classics continue to inspire, entertain and enlighten millions of readers everywhere.

'No publisher has had more influence on reading habits than Penguin'
Independent

'Penguins provided a crash course in world literature'
Guardian

The best books ever written

PENGUIN CLASSICS

SINCE 1946

Find out more at www.penguinclassics.com